An Ancient Key: Relationships

Other Books By Aubrey Dawn Weinzetl:

Held Hostage (Paperback) ISBN: 9798987989302

Held Hostage (Ebook) ISBN: 9798987989326

Beyond Held Hostage (Paperback) ISBN: 9798987989319

An Ancient Key: Relationships

Uncovering a Mystery of Old.

Aubrey Dawn Weinzetl

An Ancient Key: Relationships

By Aubrey Dawn Weinzetl

Published by Aubrey Dawn Weinzetl, Sioux Falls, SD

www.aubreydw.com

Aubrey.heldhostage@gmail.com

Neither the publisher nor the author is engaged in rendering advice or services to the individual reader. Neither the author nor the publisher shall be liable or responsible for any loss, injury, or damage allegedly arising from any information or suggestion in this book. The opinions expressed in this book represent the personal views of the author and not of the publisher, and are for informational purposes only.

Many of the various stories of people in this book draw from real life experience, at certain points involving a composite of stories. In some instances people's names have been changed in these stories to protect privacy.

ISBN: 979-8-9879893-3-3

Library of Congress Control Number: 2024904134

Editors: Krystle Van Roekel, Valerie Weinzetl, Douglas Weinzetl

Cover Layout & Images/Drawings: Aubrey Dawn Weinzetl

Book Layout: Aubrey Dawn Weinzetl

"Scripture taken from the HOLY BIBLE, (NIV) NEW INTERNATIONAL VERSION. Copyright © 1973, 1978, 1984 Biblica. Used by permission of Zondervan. All rights reserved.

Dedication

This book is dedicated to my siblings.

Austin~ Your journey held many surprises, and there were times we almost lost you, but the Father has a powerful plan for you and your family. I am excited to see what He does through you and your family, as you continue to say 'Yes,' to Him. You and your family have not arrived at the end, you have just reached a new chapter. I love you.

Aaron, Andrew, and Baby Baby~ Your journey here on earth was short, and you never had to taste the bitterness of this world, but instead you have only known the joy of the Father's embrace. I continue on my journey, until the day I am reunited with you all in Heaven in the Father's embrace. I love you all.

Alexis~ The journey the Holy Spirit has taken you on and the steps He wants you to take will empower you to live your fullest. He has continued to call you higher, and I have loved seeing how He passionately pursues you. I look forward to seeing the full impact your family's obedience will have on the world for the Father's Kingdom. I love you.

Alyssia~ Your journey has held ups and downs, led through valleys and mountaintops, and I know that the Father is not done with you. He still has a plan and calling on your life, and I look forward to seeing how He leads you on the rest of your journey. I love you.

CONTENTS

Prologue

It has been three years since my life changed. Three years since my ex-husband and I separated and then divorced. Three years through which the Father has taken me on a journey of healing, breakthrough, freedom, and restoration.

During these three years, the Father transformed my beliefs and views of the Trinity. In three years, my relationship with Them has deepened beyond what I could ever imagine was possible on this side of Heaven, and yet I know He is going to be taking me even deeper this coming year.

After writing Held Hostage and Beyond Held Hostage, I thought I was done writing. I planned on focusing more on the ministering to others part of my calling, believing that what the Father wanted me to write down and run with was complete. I should have known better.

I had just started a women's Bible Study, taking them through Beyond Held Hostage, when the Father told me that the next step after the four month Bible Study would be to write a book on relationships. I didn't fight Him on it, but I definitely questioned if I was the right person to do this. The Father had been revealing things about relationships to my spirit for three years. But when it came to actually expressing them to individuals, I struggled to put into words exactly what these blueprints looked like.

But I told the Father, 'Yes', and there was no going back. The Holy Spirit then led me to specific relationships (through different avenues such as in personal life, TV shows, etc.), all of which incorporated the new blueprints. After observing, I started writing down the different details that made them healthy ones. After putting all the details down, I asked the Father what He wanted this book to look like. Very clearly He told me, **"Aubrey, this book is going to be a journey that I will have** you and the Holy Spirit go on together. You will need to listen to Him and write down what He speaks to you. I will give you a picture of each observation and witness that you will observe, and with this picture, the Holy Spirit will reveal what you need to see and write."

Within this journey you will see the term 'Philip-Transported,' which comes from the account of transportation found in Acts 8:26-40. Although I was not physically transported, the Holy Spirit would place a picture before me, and then He would reveal what was taking place in each picture. There were times the Holy Spirit would give the information through visions, but it wasn't like the usual vision where you are transported directly into it; instead, I would watch it almost like a movie on a TV screen. I would look at my computer screen and I would watch the vision play out instead of seeing the words I was writing. Other times I would just see a picture, but then the Holy Spirit would give wisdom, knowledge, and discernment on what was taking place within that image. Sometimes there was no image at all, and instead I could hear the conversation taking place and wrote what I heard in my spirit. The Bible says that the Father, Son, and Holy Spirit have different ways of communicating with us. Ways that I experienced the Trinity's communication while on this journey were the whisper of the Father's voice and the voice of the Holy Spirit (discerning Who was speaking to me), a deep down knowing, dreams, my own life experiences, the Bible, discernment, wisdom, understanding, knowledge, prophecy, and visions. There were times where He had me prophetically write out the relationship the Father has for my nephew and nieces; and not only for them, but also for my own relationship to come. Then we would discuss it, and I would write down the Holy Spirit's and my discussion throughout the journey.

So join me on this journey of relationships, led by the Holy Spirit.

Part 1

Brother/sister-in-Christ Relationships

Chapter 1

For so long, everything has been dark. At times I would catch a glimpse of color, but it would only grow hazy again. This pitch black, unbearable darkness has clouded out all joy and life, and instead of vibrancy, there was only survival. For years I have been in this foggy darkness, just waiting to be rescued.

"Aubrey." The sound of my name being called created a feeling of warmth that had been missing from my life for so many years.

"Aubrey." The stirring to seek out who was saying my name became so strong that I immediately began to feel my way through the darkness, arms outstretched, grasping at anything and everything, trying so hard to find the one who called my name with such warmth and love.

"Who is this that is calling me? Who are you that you would recognize me?" I begged this warmth voice, hoping that my broken plea would be heard, that for once my cry would receive a response.

"Aubrey." Suddenly it was as if a spotlight shone on me. Everything around me was dark, but in this sheltered circle there was light. I could finally see that in my searching of the voice, my feet had come to stand on a diabase rock. The charcoal-colored rock contrasted with the white light surrounding me. However, the air within this circle felt fresh, and I began to smell the faint scent of a hibiscus flower. Although I couldn't see who was talking to me, I knew that He was near.

"Here I am," were the only words that I could bring myself to say. This situation had once been so normal, but now was completely foreign.

"Aubrey, these last fifteen years have been so hard for you, My child." At once the voice become familiar, and a peace settled over me. Yet with it deep pain, because I had been away from my Father for fifteen years.

"Daddy, it has been hard, and I am ready to come home."

Light exploded all around, and the darkness was vanquished. I looked down to see that I was wearing a black short sleeved dress with white plumeria flower print and black leggings. I glanced around me and saw that I was in what once was a beautiful garden, and at the center of this garden was the diabase rock I was standing on. As I looked around, I began to notice that the hibiscus flowers around me were in different stages. Some were beginning to blossom, while others were in full bloom.

"Daddy, why is there no color? Why is everything black, grey, and white? Where are the beautiful, vibrant colors I once knew?"

"These fifteen years stole so much from you, My daughter. You once were full of life and dreams, and looked forward to the future I created just for you. But the abuse, betrayal, and heartache you suffered at the hands of the one who was supposed to protect you changed who I had created you to be. Your survival mode kicked in, and every day I watched as you clung to reality by a small thread. But My precious daughter, that thread was connected to My hand, and I was not willing to ever let you go. This garden is the garden of your heart. I have protected your calling, your purpose, and the promises I have given you. But the color will be returned through your healing process."

Tears poured from my eyes as my Father's words resonated within my spirit. I knew that He was right, and I felt so very loved. My Father is the one who created me in my mother's womb. He knit me together, and within me He birthed a purpose and calling that could never be fully destroyed. My Father is the One and True God, in Israel His name is Adonai, another name is Elohim, and He is part of the Trinity. The Trinity is Adonai

(Father), Yeshua (Jesus the Son), and Ruach Hakodesh (Holy Spirit).

During the last fifteen years, I had slowly pulled away from my Father. It had become harder and harder to hear His voice, let alone trust that I actually could hear Him. Yet, at this moment I finally understood that my silent cry throughout these fifteen years was finally coming true. I was about to be rescued and delivered.

"Aubrey, I am going to be taking you through a time of healing. During this time, cling to Me even more and don't let go. As you cling to Me, you will find the vibrant colors will come back, for you will be fully alive in Me."

"Okay Daddy, let's do this!"

***

Three years later…

"Aubrey."

"Yes, Daddy!" A smile split across my lips as I heard my Father's voice.

"So many things have happened these three years. I have taken you on a beautiful healing journey, but I know that it was very painful and hard. You had to face the most evil of memories and the darkest of lies that once held you hostage. But look now at the garden of your heart."

I immediately turned to do so and I began to see that color had returned to my garden. Bright colors of blue, orange, pink, purple, yellow, green, red, in every shade and tone you could imagine surrounded me. It was so beautiful and the plants and flowers were so very lush and healthy. It stole my breath, and I had no words to express the wonder of what I was seeing. When I was finally able to gasp in a breath, my nose was assaulted with the sweet aroma of hibiscus flowers. It was so fragrant, and mixed with it was the fresh air of the prairie, clean and pure. I raised my eyes and saw the sky was crystal blue, ranging in beautiful shades of baby blue to royal blue. So much variation, so clear and bright.

"My daughter, I had you write your testimony in Held Hostage because the world needs to see My glory and My great love. The world needs to see that no matter how far one falls, I have the power to call them back if they just say, 'yes', like you did. Your testimony brings Me honor and ignites the hope in others that they too can have a future that is beyond anything they could dream. Not only did I have you write Held Hostage, but I then called you to write Beyond Held Hostage. This book was even more important than your testimony, because it shows others how to return to their First Love, ME. For within this book, I placed My heart for them, and as you wrote the words I gave you, it caused a fire of passion to return to those who listened and responded to My love. My Daughter, I have a question for you."

Smiling, I nodded. I knew that His question would require a step of obedience, but again I knew that I would say, "yes" to Him.

"Yes, Daddy."

"Do you see how your garden is a circle, and how on the outer edge we, you and I, had placed this wall of stones to create a barrier of protection?"

"Yes, I see the rock wall. It has protected my garden well."

"Yes, My daughter, it protected your garden while you healed, while you created new habits and lifestyle, and it kept you focused on My leading. It's been three years, and you have grown, you have healed, and you have put habits in place to help you overcome the past. The wall of protection did its job, but now it needs to come down."

Shock radiated through me. "Come down? Why? This wall has helped me to protect myself from making those same mistakes, from trusting the wrong people and wrong alignments, and has kept my feet on the path You have directed me on. Why must it come down?"

"My warrior daughter, what do you see happening to the hibiscus that is closest to the wall?"

I turned my eyes to where my Father directed, and I noticed that the flowers closest to the wall were still shades of gray instead of full of color and vibrancy.

"Father, why are they still gray?"

"Daughter." I could hear the smile in His voice. "The wall is no longer protecting you, but keeping you from stepping out. In order to heal and grow and leave behind the baggage of your past, the wall gave you the privacy and focus to do that. Now that you are healed, you have learned habits to help with your post-traumatic stress disorder, and now know the right way of having a relationship; the wall is keeping you from moving forward into all that I have for you."

I knew my Daddy was right. "But Daddy, I am scared to let the wall come down."

"Why?" His reply was so gentle. I knew He knew the reason even before I opened my mouth, but I also knew He was waiting for my honesty.

"Because when the wall comes down, the longing for a spouse will come back. Daddy, that longing led me into a place of death eighteen years ago. I pushed ahead of You and made a marriage happen, but it was the worst thing I could have done. For I chose one who was not willing to heal and grow with You. Instead, he betrayed me with his affairs and abandoned me. He hurt me with his emotional, spiritual, mental, and sexual abuse. Although I know that I am healed and have grown, I'm scared that when the longing is birthed again, I will make the same decision."

"Daughter, everything that I have done in you and with you forever changed how you will respond to the longing. There is no reason to fear the longing. The truth is, Aubrey, you are not scared of the longing, but you are scared of being hurt again. You are scared that the one I bring you will not want you and will hurt you the same way as your ex-husband. But Daughter, fear is not of me. For My love casts out all fear."

I slowly took in my Father's words, and again I knew He was right. I was scared of being hurt again, but I also knew that this time would be different, because my Daddy was the one bringing us together.

"Okay Daddy, let's take down the wall and let the longing in."

"Aubrey." Once more, I heard His smile and felt His joy over my obedience. "To start the process of tearing down the wall, you are going to go on a journey to see all that you have learned in these three years. Not only that, but I am going to give you insight into what I am doing now throughout the earth in all relationships. For I am bringing a new oil to relationships. This new blueprint will affect brother and sister relationships, dating and engaged relationships, and finally, marriage and family relationships."

"Ummmm....are you sure I'm the one to do this? I mean, this is heavy stuff."

"Yes, you are to do it, but you won't be alone. The Holy Spirit will be leading you on this journey. I have given Him the direction and the paths to take you on, so listen very closely to what He speaks."

Peace settled around me.

"I understand. I will listen to what the Holy Spirit says, and follow Your leading."

In an instance I was Philip-Transported into a room full of people...

Chapter 2

The noise levels were insanely loud, and I felt a bit overwhelmed by the sudden amount of people surrounding me. My heart was pounding after the quick Philip-Transport, and I realized I might need to get used to it, especially if the Holy Spirit was going to be using this form of transportation a lot. I took deep breaths as I quickly fixed my purple hair and pulled it up into a ponytail. After straightening my dress, I slowly began to adjust to the noise levels and to observe the individuals in the room. There were men and women, young and old, all just talking and mingling together. It was an interesting place to begin my journey because I am more of an introvert, and so being in this crowd caused me to rely on my Father's strength. I knew, though, that it was an important detail the Holy Spirit was leading me to, because in the midst of the crowd a young man stood out to me.

He appeared to be in his later teenage years, soon to graduate and enter the adult world. He was tall, well-built, and his appearance was boyishly handsome. Yet beyond his outward appearance, his dark blue eyes held a mysterious hint that all was not okay.

"Aubrey?"

I stilled myself in the noisy room, calming my spirit and taking note of the Holy Spirit.

"Yes, Holy Spirit."

"In this journey, I am going to open your eyes to what others do not see. I am going to open your ears so that you can hear the thoughts of the individuals I reveal to you. On the first leg of the journey, we are going to focus on brother and sister relationships in Christ. Many who have come into the family of God are unsure of what these new relationships are meant to look like. Sadly, in most church families, what they find is not the new blueprint that the Father has in store for them. I am going to start with this young man here."

Immediately we were Philip-Transported to a bedroom. This time I was somewhat prepared for the jolt, and thankfully my hair was already pulled back. I looked around as I fixed my dress, and noticed the walls were green, with pictures of famous football players plastered on them. There was a queen-size bed with forest green sheets tossed around in disarray. Clothes were strewn across the floor, and the dresser drawers could barely close with even more threatening to tumble out. There was a large, black L-shape desk in front of the bed that connected to the left side of the room. On one part of the desk there appeared to be a gaming center with all the controls and equipment ready for use. On the other side was a computer and schoolbooks for studying. As I looked quietly around the room, I heard the sound of the doorknob turning. I quickly moved to the wall, unsure if whoever was coming in would be able to see me, or if I was invisible to them. The idea of asking the Holy Spirit didn't even come to mind as I watched with a mix of fear and excitement.

"He cannot see you." I jumped at the sound of the Holy Spirit's voice, and giggled at how He knew me so well.

"Starting now, I want you to observe David and the relationship he has with his sisters in Christ."

I nodded silently.

The next second the door burst open.

"Mom, I'm going to finish my homework now because some of my friends from youth group are hanging out tonight. I think we're going to go watch a movie."

"Okay, David."

David shut his door and locked it. It had become a customary thing for his family to know that when he was doing homework, he would lock his door so he wouldn't be interrupted. David pulled out his homework and turned on his computer. He began to research swimmer athletes for a paper he was writing for English. His teacher had asked them to write an essay on a sport they are not familiar with, and pick an athlete of that sport that they came to admire while researching the new sport.

As David began to research, he decided it would be fun to choose a woman athlete. He knew how the world had been trying to strip women from who God had created them to be, and that even within their own sport, they were forced to compete with men who identified as women.

I really respected the women athletes who were standing up and bringing recognition to how this was all wrong.

While David surfed the web for the right athlete, he started to get distracted by the women in their swimming suits. Trying to push down the surge of desire rushing through his body, he began to write down the information he was finding. But the urges of lust had a mind of their own, and soon David was searching for porn featuring women as athletes. Continuing to watch, David got up from his chair and went to his bed.

BAM!! My head jerked from the quick Philip-Transportation the Holy Spirit had just brought me on. This one took a bit of time to get over. I closed my eyes to keep from being overcome by nausea. After many deep breaths I realized that now I found myself in a Chinese restaurant, and sitting before me was David and a female who appeared to be around the same age as him. She had dark wavy brown hair, dark brown eyes, she was thin, and her skin had a warm glow. You could tell that she enjoyed sunning. She wore the in-style of short shorts and she had on a tight tank top. As I watched, I could tell that David was struggling. The look in his eyes revealed that he had something important to discuss with the girl. Once again the Holy Spirit nudged me, and I knew He wanted me to observe again.

"Becca?"

"Yeah."

"We have been friends for a couple of years now. You are one of my closest friends and you have been there for me during my darkest of days when my dad died. I've been wanting to talk to you about something that's, well, it's been on my mind for awhile. I hope you will be okay with me talking to you about it?"

"Sure, you know I am here for you. Besides, we told each other we would always be honest with one another."

"Remember how five months ago I told you I had been struggling with lust, and how one of my guy friends on my football team got me watching porn?"

"Yeah, I know that you have been trying to overcome it. We pray about it all the time and we have talked about what habits you could put in place to keep yourself from, well, pleasuring yourself. Has it been helping?"

"Yes and no. It kind of depends. Some days I feel like I have completely overcome the temptation to watch porn and pleasure myself, and then a bad day comes and I fall into it so quickly. It can be discouraging at times."

"I'm sorry. I know that has been really hard for you. Have you thought more about talking to our youth pastor about it?"

"Yeah, I actually talked with him last week."

"That is awesome. What did he say?"

"Well, I shared with him how sometimes I have a really hard time being around the girls in our Bible Study because of how they dress and because I am trying to break free from lust, porn, and pleasuring myself, at times they've become a hindrance to that freedom."

David watched Becca's reaction and wondered if she would catch on to what he was saying. His heart started to pound faster. He was about to be really honest with her. In the last year Becca had begun to wear more revealing clothes. Sometimes her stomach would show, or her shorts would be so short that you could see parts of her bottom, and then other times her clothes were so tight that every bit of her beautiful figure was revealed.

Becca grew a bit quiet and watched David closely.

"I don't really know how to say this, but I'm just going to be honest with you. Do you think that when we are together you could, um…change the style of clothing you wear?"

A hardness came into Becca's eyes, and fear grew in David's heart.

"I'm sorry, but why does your struggle mean that I need to change? You are the one with the problem, and you should be working on getting your mind renewed. I shouldn't have to change what I wear because I should have the freedom to wear what I want. You should be in charge of getting yourself free from porn and masturbation." Anger dripped from her tongue as she spoke, and each word was like daggers flying at David's heart.

He flinched back. "Well…I mean I just thought since we were such good friends you would want to help me."

"Help you…I help you by praying for you and encouraging you. Me changing my style and what I wear forces me to change when I shouldn't need to. It's your problem, not mine. It's my body. You don't see guys having to watch what they wear."

David remained silent. He was having a hard time putting to words the pain he was feeling at her words. He felt judged and condemned by her, his closest friend.

"You know David, I think I need some space from you. When you have gotten freedom from this, then give me a call and we can hangout then. 'Kay?"

"Um, sure, Becca. I understand."

Once again I was Philip-Transported away, but this time I found myself in a park.

Chapter 3

I couldn't forget David's eyes that were filled with pain, nor Becca's that flashed in anger. I began to ponder what I had just observed, and it took me a second to recognize that I was at a park and that this time, I had no reaction to the transportation. I realized that there were bike trails, and they were following a river that flowed steadily by.

"Aubrey, you just observed a painful reality that many brothers and sisters in Christ have experienced. David and Becca grew up together. In fact, their family ties were so strong that they considered each other's families a second home. They grew up playing together, celebrating holidays and birthdays together, and they grew up sharing all their personal feelings, thoughts, and problems with each other. Becca's dad took on the role of a second father when David's dad passed away three years earlier. In everyone's eyes, they appear to be the perfect example of a brother and sister in Christ."

I nodded along as the Holy Spirit spoke to me, but I had a nagging feeling I was missing something.

"Aubrey, go ahead and walk along this path, and as you walk I want you to process what you saw. When you reach the playground, you will find the next group I want you to observe. Be watchful, I'm sure you will know which ones I want you to pay attention too."

"Okay, Holy Spirit, I will obey."

I began to follow the path leading south along the river. I couldn't see much past the trees, for it was summer and the trees had not lost their leaves yet. I could feel the sun's heat upon my back, and I appreciated the shade from the trees. I could tell that further down there was a turn in the path, veering left. As I continued down the path, my mind wandered away from the sights and back to what I had just observed. My heart really ached for David, but I also understood Becca's response. In fact, through the years, I had heard many women say a similar thing, and I began to wonder what was the way this situation should have been handled. It's not like we can keep changing ourselves to please everyone, but at the same time, are there some things that we are to let go of for the best of others?

I finally reached the bend in the path and as I followed it left, I saw the playground up ahead. It sat perfectly in a circle of trees. There were pine trees, maple trees, and ash trees enclosing the playground. Next to it there was a sand volleyball court, where a group of men and women probably in their mid-twenties were playing. They were the closest to the outline of trees.

I walked closer, sensing the Holy Spirit nudging me in their direction. I began to silently observe, wondering who I was supposed to notice.

"Peter, hit the ball towards me this time, I want a chance to hit it."

"Sure Amy, I'll send it your way next."

Back and forth the ball was sent from one side to the other. This group of friends had been playing volleyball since they were in their high school youth group together. It had been five years since they graduated from high school, and most of them had also graduated from college. They had become a close group of friends, and now, since they were too old for youth group they had created a small life group.

"Hey Peter, I'm going to get a drink of water. Are you good playing a man down?"

"No problem, Ham. We got this." The group laughed.

"Hey Ham, can I join you? I could really use some water and a break."

Ham nodded, "Sure thing, Delila."

Ham and Delila made their way closer to where I had sat down to observe. Grabbing their water bottles, they settled on the ground under the shade of the tree closest to me. My ears perked up as I listened in on their conversation, ignoring the sweltering heat.

"Wow, I am tired. I can't believe the others have so much energy." Delila sighed, taking a drink before lying flat on the ground. "My muscles are shaking, and my heart feels like it's going a hundred miles an hour."

Ham smiled at her exaggeration. "I bet, we used to play volleyball every week, and now it's once a month."

"That's true. Life got way too busy for us all, didn't it?"

"Yeah, I have four years left of residency and then I can finally move to the hospital I've been dreaming of working at. Seems I get fewer chances to hangout with you. Church has been harder to make as well."

"I hear ya, I am so busy working at the hotel. They just promoted me to manager and it seems like the turnover rate is never ending. I always get called in to work on my scheduled days off."

Ham nodded in understanding. Life sure had brought changes that most of the friends hadn't been prepared for. But Ham was thankful that even though they couldn't make it to most Sundays, at least they were able to connect once a month playing volleyball.

After a while Ham took his eyes off the game and looked down at Delila who was lying down next to him. He was surprised to find her looking at him.

"Ham, I just noticed that you have really piercing eyes. Not like you are glaring at people, but it's like you can see further into people's thoughts."

Ham laughed. "Hmmm…I have been told that, but I guess I just feel like it's normal." Ham took a minute to look closer at Delila. "Has anyone ever told you that you have bedroom eyes?"

Delila looked surprised, "Bedroom eyes?"

Ham nodded. "Yeah, bedroom eyes, eyes that pull a guy in, signaling you want to go to bed with him."

Delila sat up in surprise. "I have never been told that before. Is that really what my eyes show?"

Ham nodded, "It's very subtle, but yeah, they have this dreamy pull to them."

Delila sat quietly, thinking about Ham's words. She wasn't quite sure what to make of his statement. She definitely didn't want to be intimate with him, so why did he feel as if her eyes was giving off that vibe? Lost in thought, she didn't notice Ham shifting closer to her.

"Delila?"

Delila jumped before she focused back on him. Finding him a little too close for comfort, she moved her head back a bit.

"Yeah."

"I was just thinking about this hilarious situation that happened to a co-worker at work. Would you like to hear it?"

"Oh, sure, I love funny work situations."

Ham was laughing before he even started the story. It was really too hilarious to put into words, but he just had to share. "So there's a female doctor who's also doing her residency with me. Yesterday, when we were on duty, she went into this old man's room, and he had the best joke for her."

Ham started laughing again. "Okay, sorry, let me catch my breath. So here is the joke and my coworker's response. An old man and a younger woman met in a bar, but ended up at a hotel for a one-night stand. How many times was the old man able to have sex that night? My co-worker paused for a bit and then said, 'Once?' The old man laughed and then answered, 'None, my heart started acting up before we could even get started.' The old man laughed and laughed, and my co-worker was so embarrassed. Then he leaned over and said, 'How about you and I have a night together instead?'" Ham started laughing again, barely able to catch his breath.

Delila started to giggle. "Your co-worker must have been so confused about what to do."

"She escaped his room faster than a runaway train. So what about you, Delila, want to spend a crazy night with an old man?"

Delila laughed uncomfortably at the question. "No, I'm good…your co-worker can have him." Delila and Ham continued to laugh at the 'hilarious situation' that his co-worker had found herself in.

I sat quietly, listening to their teasing. And slowly Ham started teasing Delila and telling her more sexual jokes. Slowly Delila's laughs began to become real and less awkward. However, listening in on these jokes was giving me a strong uneasiness in my belly.

"Aubrey, go ahead and continue your walk. You have observed enough of their brother/sister relationship."

I breathed a sigh of relief. "Thank You, Holy Spirit. I don't think I could have sat there any longer. I was feeling so uncomfortable."

As I got up and moved away, I knew in my spirit that my Father was happy that it made me uncomfortable and that I didn't want to stay around and listen to it anymore.

"Aubrey, it's time for Me to transport you to our next observation."

"Alright, let's do it."

Chapter 4

With that, I was Philip-Transported into a dark room. Slowly, the lights in front of me came on. I realized I was in a traditional theater hall with red chairs and rich wood tones throughout the space, and a group of friends were standing on the stage the lights illuminated. The space wasn't large, only big enough to hold maybe an audience of a hundred. The chairs were situated in a half circle, and the floor sloped down toward the stage in a layering look, giving all the audience members clear viewing.

I looked around me and noticed that no one else was sitting in the audience seats, and it also didn't appear that the group of twenty-five members was performing right now. I began observing the group to find out what exactly they were up to.

"Alright everyone, quiet down, the owner has some words for us before we begin figuring out our roles for the new play," the director encouraged. Everyone grew silent as they watched the owner come forward.

"Good evening, everyone," he said.

"Good evening," everyone echoed.

"When I first started Kingdom Theaters thirty years ago, I never imaged how God would use this theater to spread the Gospel and reveal His love to the lost. You have all been with me for eight years now, all of you joining right after college. You're in your thirties now, and I find God's humor in the fact that the cast right now are in their early thirties too. I feel strongly that this next play, based on the life of Ruth, is going to be a powerful experience for the audience members. They will be able to connect with an amazing woman from the Bible and perhaps they will understand the courage Ruth showed and see they can also have courage as life gets harder."

The performers smiled and nodded in agreement. The owner continued. "In the western world we have begun to see the evidence of things becoming harder for believers, and as the End

Times will eventually come, we want to encourage believers to remain strong in the Lord. So as you work with the producer and figure out your parts, keep in mind that everything you are doing is for God's glory. I know you are all a very close-knit family here at Kingdom Theaters, so let's work together as the family of God to bring His kingdom here."

"Amen!" Everyone shouted together and smiled. They watched as the owner left and soon the director made his way to the front of the stage.

I watched closely, trying to figure out who I was supposed to be observing. There was someone I was supposed to be watching more than the rest, wasn't there?

"Aubrey."

"Yes?" I smiled knowing that the Holy Spirit was about to answer what I had inwardly asked.

"I want you to observe the lady in the deep royal blue dress."

"Got it. I'm on it, Holy Spirit."

Immediately I began to observe her. I noticed that she had beautiful straight, full black hair, olive skin, and her facial features hinted at her Italian ancestry.

Anna had been in theater since she was a little girl. Her father was an actor and her mother belonged to a Christian contemporary music group. Between the two, Anna loved theater. In theater she could both sing and act, which was the best of both worlds. However, Anna had never been given the opportunity to sing as a lead. She always had confidence when singing a choir part, but to have the whole song was something she really longed for. Anna had been practicing for months now, building up her confidence to sing alone.

Anna turned her head to look at her good friend Brandon. He had been so encouraging when she had told him she wanted to try for the lead role of Ruth and sing the solo. Brandon noticed that she was watching and smiled, giving her a thumbs up in encouragement.

"Okay everyone, it's time to start the tryouts for different parts so we can get the cast list finalized." The director motioned for everyone to take a seat and get ready. "We have the three main leads, Naomi, Ruth, and Boaz. The rest of the cast will be divided up as Orpah, a closer kinsman redeemer, friends of Naomi, and then workers in the field, etc. All three main leads will each have one solo song, and then have a couple songs together. I think we will start out with Ruth and narrow down who will play her. If you would like a chance at her part, please come to the front."

Again Anna looked at Brandon, and with his nod of approval she decided to do something new that she had never done before: sing a solo. Anna walked up to the front where two of her friends were also waiting to try out. They all exchanged excited and encouraging smiles.

"All right ladies, I am going to have each of you read through a scene, and then I would like you to sing the chorus to the solo song."

The three friends nodded in agreement.

"Who would like to go first?" The director looked towards Anna's right, where Jessica stood. She had been a lead many times and confidently sang the solos. She had played Esther in the last play they performed.

Jessica smiled at the director. "I will go first."

Anna and her other friend Morgan walked to the left side of the stage to watch Jessica perform. Anna kept her eyes down as she listened to Jessica perform flawlessly. Doubts as to what she was doing began to creep in, and Anna reminded herself that at home she was able to hit every note right on beat, and even her parents had said she sounded so beautiful. Taking deep breaths,

Anna silently encouraged herself.

Thunderous applause assailed Anna, who realized Jessica was done with her audition. Before Anna could say a word, Morgan shouted out, "Director, I would like to go next!"

"Alright Morgan, go ahead."

Anna watched as Morgan took center stage. She was full of joy and excitement. Her song carried happy enthusiasm, whereas Jessica had made it sound soulful. Anna wondered how she should sing. Once again, applause erupted around Anna and she knew that it was her turn. Anna raised her eyes to look at the director and timidly said, "I would like to go now, director." "

"Alright Anna, come audition for the part of Ruth."

Jessica and Morgan smiled at her from stage left.

Anna carefully made her way to center stage. She started her lines, flawlessly delivering a passionate plea for Naomi to let her go to Israel with her. The director nodded in approval. Anna took a deep breath. It was time for the song. "I can do this." Anna said quietly to herself. The music started, and nerves hit Anna like a wave. As she began to sing her voice came out timidly and she found herself struggling to even pronounce the words correctly. Her breathing became a bit labored, but she continued to push through. Halfway through the chorus Anna forgot the next word, and when she finally remembered it, her voice came out squeaky and off-beat. She stopped singing altogether and looked down, afraid to look at anyone and see their disapproval. Her face flushed red from the embarrassment.

"That was a good try, Anna. I think we should practice some more and audition for the lead in the next play, okay?"

Anna nodded her head at the director, and turned to walk back to her friends waiting on stage right.

"Anna, that was hilarious. I videotaped your squeaky voice, I can't believe I got it on film!" Brandon shouted out. Everyone around him started laughing. "Hey, you gave it a shot, and boy you made everyone's day a little more enjoyable." Everyone else laughed harder. Anna kept her eyes on the ground, but her heart was shocked by Brandon's response and words.

"Hey Drew, what did you think of Anna's audition?" Brandon asked merrily.

"Oh it was something. I'm not really sure why you tried out Anna, you know Jessica is the best we have for solo singing. Morgan is a close second. You're nowhere near their field. But I am glad you did, because I really needed the laugh."

Drew's words hit Anna's heart like arrows. Anna raised her eyes to see all of her friends laughing and teasing her. "Can you believe she wanted to try out?" "I know, why try and go against Jessica? She is amazing." "Anna, you should really stick with the things you are confident and good at. God only calls the equipped, so stay in the field He equipped you for."

Anna felt hurt. Her friends had no idea the amount of courage it had taken her to get up and audition. She had had to overcome her fear, and yet all they cared about was the laughter it brought them at her expense. Anna looked down again, willing her tears not to fall.

I sadly watched on, my heart breaking at the situation unfolding. As an introvert, I had been there before. Being bold and courageous were not a part of my vocabulary growing up. In fact, shy and socially awkward probably fit best. I tried to calm my heart, but I felt just as embarrassed as Anna, and yet I understood how brave she had just been.

"Aubrey, it's time for the next observation. Are you ready or do you need a minute?"

I took a deep breath and calmed myself. "No, I'm good. Let's go now, Holy Spirit."

Chapter 5

It wasn't long before I found myself Philip-Transported to an apartment complex's swimming pool. There were kids, young adults, and older adults hanging out around the edge of the pool, watching others playing in the pool. There were only about twenty individuals in total, but the fun of the pool was deafening to those walking by.

I watched on for a couple of minutes till my gaze settled on a group of adults sitting around a table fire pit. The sun was beginning to set, and soon the pool would be closing. Steam was coming off the heated pool, and slowly parents were collecting their children to go in for the day. The group of six remained.

"Holy Spirit, they are the ones You want me to observe, aren't they?"

"**Good job, you are beginning to sense My leading stronger, where words are not necessary. You sense the Father's peace.**"

I smiled because it was true. I had come to know my Father's voice and the Holy Spirit's leading, so I was beginning to understand when the peace stayed with me, and when it wasn't there.

I pulled my eyes back to the group and began to observe their playful banter.

There were six friends hanging out, but out of the six friends, five of them had known each other since middle school. They had belonged to a Christian private school and with smaller-sized classes, they had learned to rely on one another. For fifteen years they had supported one another and encouraged each other in their walk with God. Out of all the friends, there was one who had only joined them recently. Kanoa had become good friends with Ariella, having met her at work, and the rest of the group welcomed him in with warm smiles.

Kanoa was a character. With his dark brown eyes, black hair, tan skin, and athletic build it was no surprise that he was a hit among women. He enjoyed making others laugh, he was outgoing, and was a popular athlete in high school. He enjoyed sports, and although he had been saved for quite a few years, he was still learning how to walk out his relationship with God.

Ariella was the complete opposite. Sports were not her strength, and she took life very seriously. She loved coloring her hair, but that was as outgoing as she got. She was the more quiet and observant type, and was completely aware of everything going on around her. Today her curly hair was purple, and it brought out the shine of her blue eyes. Ariella was also sensitive; she was hyperaware of the emotions and feelings of others. Sometimes she had sensory overload when her own emotions and others were combined, creating a heavy sensation through her whole body.

Today was one of those days, where Ariella was working hard to maintain her peace of mind. Aaron, Abraham, Andrew, and Stephanie had always been a great support for Ariella. They understood her sensory overload, and over the years had become comfortable with her tears. They never judged her or told her she needed to buck up. Instead, they had worked together to create habits that Ariella could apply when she was feeling overwhelmed. Usually, Ariella would go away for a bit and let the silence seep into her noisy head, but today, with being outside, there wasn't anywhere to go to escape the noise levels of the kids in the pool.

Ariella felt pressured too, because Kanoa had just recently started hanging out with the group, and she knew that the rest of the group was still getting comfortable with him.

"Hey, how about we go to my house for a late night snack?" Aaron asked the group. The others nodded, while Kanoa stayed quiet.

"Sounds good to me," Stephanie joined in.

"Alright, let's all head over now, and I'll order food so it's ready when we get there."

"Sounds good. I'll ride with Kanoa since he hasn't been to your place before," Ariella said, deciding that would be best course of action. Kanoa remained silent until they got into the car.

"Well Holy Spirit, are we joining them?"

"Yes, Aubrey. I want you to observe what takes place with Ariella and Kanoa. Wherever they go I want you to follow them." I nodded my head and was Philip-Transported to the backseat of Kanoa's GMC pearl Sierra.

"Hey, it sounded like Aaron was going to order some pizza," said Kanoa. "I'm hungry for a hamburger so let's go get one and then head over."

Ariella felt uncomfortable, but she understood Kanoa might not want pizza. Hopefully they wouldn't be too late, because the rest would be waiting for her to start eating. They had made it a goal to always wait for one another and eat together when they had their gatherings. "Sure, we can make it quick."

Kanoa drove to his favorite hamburger restaurant, which took fifteen minutes to get to. It was your traditional, all-American hamburger joint, with a red, white, and blue theme. They had a large selection of different hamburgers to choose from. When they arrived, he got out. "Ariella, hurry up. I'm hungry."

Ariella looked at Kanoa surprised. She had assumed they would just get his hamburger to go and wasn't prepared for him to eat inside. "Um…can you get it to go, so the rest of the group isn't waiting for us?"

"No, they don't have carry-out. Let's go." Kanoa was beginning to sound annoyed.

Ariella got out, but once they entered the restaurant she knew it was a mistake. The noise levels were intense and she began to get a headache. Not only that, but her guilt at making her friends wait was beginning to pull on her.

"Um…are you sure you can't eat a hamburger from a carry-out restaurant?"

"Ariella, stop it. We will only be here for twenty minutes and then we can go."

Ariella's emotions were beginning to rise. She quickly sent a text notifying the group that they would be a bit late and to go on and eat. Stephanie messaged back asking if everything was okay. Ariella breathed deeply as she typed out, 'Yeah, Kanoa was too hungry so he is getting food and then we will come.'

Twenty minutes later, the food finally arrived. Kanoa took his time eating and Ariella had reached her top level of sensory overload.

"Ariella, can you get over yourself? Your friends will be fine," Kanoa roughly demanded. Ariella looked around in surprise as individuals sitting at the closest tables to them looked at her.

Ariella couldn't help it, the tears came of their own free will. She had tried so hard for hours to hold them in, but they weren't having it. Kanoa's harshness was the last straw.

"Seriously? Why are you crying? You don't need to cry, you aren't a baby."

The tears fell harder and Ariella turned her head to look out the window so the rest of the restaurant couldn't see her. Humiliation flooded over her, and she fought against the embarrassment.

"Let's go, I'm not having any more fun now." Kanoa got up and left without waiting for Ariella. Ariella quickly rose and rushed to follow him to the car.

I sat in the restaurant watching the scene play out. I observed the sympathetic eyes that followed Ariella as she hurried out.

Many ladies were shaking their heads.

"I am glad that I am married to you, love, and that I don't ever have to worry about being humiliated like that," one woman told her husband, who watched Kanoa get into his car and drive away with Ariella. He nodded. "He doesn't understand the heart of a woman," he said sadly.

"Aubrey, we have another brother and sister relationship I want you to observe. Are you ready?"

"Okay, I am ready."

Chapter 6

I found myself Philip-Transported to a condo, where people were making their way home after work. I loved how it was becoming easier to sense when I was about to be transported. My connection to the Holy Spirit was becoming stronger. I began to listen silently to see if I had a peace about the direction I sensed the Holy Spirit leading me to. There was a younger man and woman walking ahead of me in the hallway who looked old enough to be about to graduate from college.

The man was saying hi to his neighbors as they walked by, and eventually they reached the door of his condo and they went inside. I observed the reaction of the neighbors around them, who were glancing at the closed door. "I wonder if she is the new girlfriend, and if she is planning on staying the night," one male neighbor chuckled to another.

I gave the closed door a thoughtful look. "Okay, take me in, Holy Spirt."

Instantly I was inside the condo, into the living room where they were sitting on the sectional talking. I began to observe.

The living room was spacious, with lots of natural light. The walls had been painted eggshell white, and the walnut laminate flooring created an inviting feel to the space. Pictures of wildlife were displayed on the walls, along with a big screen tv. The furniture was bulky and manly, like something you would find in a man cave.

Elizabeth and Taemin had met at the church singles group that they had been going to for a couple of years. But in the last couple of months, they had been talking more.

"Thank you so much, Taemin, for being willing to hear me out and give me your opinion. I really want a male perspective, and I know that your walk with God is strong."

Taemin smiled at Elizabeth. "You're welcome. I know what

it's like to be in a place of doubt and struggling and needing counsel from someone else."

Elizabeth smiled back, thinking about how she was going to share her story. Her story began six years ago, when she was just sixteen years old. It seemed like an eternity ago. When she was sixteen she had fallen in love with the most popular guy in school. A month later they were dating. Six weeks later, she gave him her virginity. She never expected that the next day he would move on to his next target, and that just four weeks after that she would find out that she was pregnant.

Elizabeth could still remember those painful months as the whole school judged her, and, when she refused to get an abortion, how the popular ex-boyfriend made up gossip about her and spread it through the school. She went from being invisible to most hated in one day. Her parents moved her to a different town and to a new school where no one knew her story, just that she was a pregnant teen mom. The hardest decision she ever had to make was one done in love. She gave up her daughter for adoption. She knew the couple, and had seen their love for God and how they had been waiting five years to get pregnant. She knew her daughter would be loved, wanted, and raised to love God with all her heart.

Elizabeth began to share her story with Taemin. She opened up and gave him all the details, some probably weren't necessary and too intimate to share, but she felt it was needed to understand her full story and what made her give up her daughter.

Taemin listened patiently, his heart breaking at what she had gone through at such a young age.

"So I have met someone I am interested in and he recently told me that he was interested in me too, and asked me to pray about him pursuing me. I guess I am wondering when I should share this with him? I don't want him to abandon me, but I also know that he should at some point know about this?"

Taemin nodded in understanding. "Let's take some time to

pray and then I will let you know what I think?"

"Okay, sounds good."

I watched quietly as they began to pray. Their hearts were so open to God, it kind of surprised me. So far in all my observations, I had a deep knowing that there was something off, but I couldn't see what it was. Before I could hear Taemin's answer, the Holy Spirit Philip-Transported me back outside the condo door. I looked at the cedar door in surprise. "Um...Holy Spirit, why am I back outside?"

"Watch."

I kept my eyes wide open and looked around. I then noticed the two neighbors from before walking down the hall. They were around the same age as Taemin and Elizabeth. As they got close to Taemin's door, the one on the right spoke up. "It's 12am and she is still inside." He smirked at his friend. The friend smiled back, "You know what that means?" He said. "It's going to be a fun night." They walked away, laughing.

The off feeling returned in a flood as I watched them walk back to their own condo.

"Aubrey, before we go to the next observation, I want us to take time to talk through what you have observed and what the Father is wanting to show you."

"That would be great, Holy Spirit, because I have so many things running through my mind and I would love Your wisdom and insight."

"Come with Me."

I followed the Holy Spirit's leading, and He took me outside the condo complex and over to the common grounds where tables surrounded a water fountain. Each table had a fire pit. I sat down close to the fountain and took a deep breath.

"Aubrey, I would like to hear what you observed. I want you to wait on David and Becca. We will talk about them later. First, tell Me about Ham and Delila."

"So with Ham and Delila, it looked like they were super comfortable with the other, and they weren't worried about what each other thought. Like they were confident in being themselves. However, I found their teasing and jokes really inappropriate. Not just as friends, but also because they claim to be believers."

"You are right. Sadly, many in the church, married, dating, and single, have let go of constraint and now openly rejoice in sin. You might find that a bold statement, but the fact is that jokes about sexual immorality, etc., is exactly one of the sins that Jesus died for. And yet those He died for are making His pain, His sacrifice, into a joke. They are laughing at sin, and bringing it into their conversations. The Father said in Proverbs 16:28 (NIV), '[28] A perverse person stirs up conflict, and a gossip separates close friends.' He wants the speech of His children to be pure, holy, as they are a witness of Him to this world."

I nodded as my understanding grew. "You are right, I have noticed even in myself that I have become used to hearing such jokes in the world we live in. It's everywhere, but that doesn't mean we should laugh and share the jokes with others. Instead, if we are found laughing we should take that as a red flag that we are not walking in accordance with truth."

"Exactly. If you noticed, Ham and Delila had become so busy with work that they no longer went to church. That also meant that their alone time with Father each day was affected. And the less they filled themselves up with the Father, the more they filled up with the world. In fact, the Father warns His children not to give up meeting together (Hebrews 10:24-25)."

"I understand, Holy Spirit. Although they could be themselves and talk comfortably with one another, they forgot that we are the Father's ambassadors to the world and that our speech shows what is hidden in our hearts (Matthew 15:10)."

"Good job, Aubrey. That is an excellent observation. Their hearts were showing that deep down, they weren't choosing Jesus. Their actions and words were not in line with the truth. As brothers and sisters, it is very important to encourage one another in walking with the Lord. I love what the Father said in 1 Peter 1:22 (NIV), '22 Now that you have purified yourselves by obeying the truth so that you have sincere love for each other, love one another deeply, from the heart.' So what are your observations of Anna and Brandon?"

"Wow! Ummm...that one hurt, Holy Spirit. I could feel Anna's pain like it was my own. In fact, I once experienced something so very similar, just in a different context. It reminded me of how I felt in my own situation. Anna was being brave, she was trying something new, and although she knew singing solo was not a strength, she still felt the calling to do it and she obeyed the Father. Brandon, however, made her obedience into a joke. He got the rest of their friends to join in and ridicule her for trying something new."

"You are right. Instead of protecting his sister, he ended up bringing great harm to her. Job 6:14 (NIV) says, '14 "Anyone who withholds kindness from a friend forsakes the fear of the Almighty."' Instead of showing kindness to her, he ended up allowing satan to use him to do his dirty work. Would you like to hear more about their story?"

"Yes, I want to know what happened to her."

"After we left, the teasing continued for a couple more minutes. The director finally stepped in to bring everyone's attention back to Jessica and Morgan and told the group that Jessica would be playing Ruth. Although everyone moved on like nothing had happened. Anna could not. She felt completely humiliated and alone. She questioned if she had really heard the Father telling her to step out and try something new.

"What no one else knew is that the theater owner had actually been observing the whole situation. He was not impressed or happy. As he began to pray about how to handle the situation, the Father gave him a vision. In the vision, Anna was singing a solo song, and the anointing was upon her. Then he heard the Father directing him to hire a voice tutor to help Anna overcome her fears and reach her calling.

"After everyone left, the owner called Anna and told her what he had decided to do. At first, Anna fought it. After her experience and humiliation, Anna wanted to give up the dream. But after some encouragement, she agreed. For eight months she practiced and met with the tutor weekly. She grew and her voice became stronger. The tutor and owner would take her to different church activities where they would have her sing solo, getting her comfortable. After her eight months of tutoring, Anna no longer needed training and was walking confidently in her gifting. One day, the Father directed her to write a song about His son, Yeshua.

The owner heard it and immediately told the director that at the Christmas program, Mary would be singing a solo song written by Anna.

"The day came for the audition, and Anna walked onstage, comfortable for the first time. When she finished the chorus of her song, her fellow performers gave her a round of applause with tears streaming from their eyes. That Christmas they had to add more dates for their program, because hundreds of people were calling for tickets. Each night was packed, and every time Anna's song that she wrote about Yeshua was sung, God's anointing flooded the room. The owner would hold altar calls after each performance and over a hundred individuals gave their hearts to Jesus. Later, when the group got together after Christmas, the owner shared with them the full story starting from the pain they caused. All the performers asked Anna to forgive them; they recognized that they had become a stumbling block, and worse, they were used by satan to discourage the plan God had for Anna's life. Anna forgave them because she understood what the Father meant in 1 John 4:20-21 (NIV) which says, '[20] Whoever claims to love God yet hates a brother or sister is a liar. For whoever does not love their brother and sister, whom they have seen, cannot love God, whom they have not seen. [21] And he has given us this command: Anyone who loves God must also love their brother and sister.'

"When everyone had made their end right, the Father began to use Kingdom Theaters like never before. The music and plays they wrote and performed brought about salvations and the revealing of God's glory."

"Wow! I love that Anna didn't give up her calling. I had

once given up mine, but the Father lovingly brought me back into truth and realignment. I'm so thankful He did."

"Exactly, imagine what would have happened if the owner hadn't stepped in. The performers would have prevented people from being saved and the glory of the Father from being revealed. I praise the Father that the owner listened and responded to My leading. But imagine how many individuals there are who have missed out on their callings and seeing God bring others to heaven, because their brother or sister tore down the very thing God was doing?"

I nodded in agreement and tears fell down my face. To know that something good had come out of such a painful moment filled me with great joy, but to know there were many missed opportunities and failures of others in the church broke my heart.

"Now for the last one, Elizabeth and Taemin. What did you observe?"

"Hmmm...that one was hard. I think it was important for Elizabeth to have Taemin's perspective and it seemed like he was really taking time to listen to what You would say. But something felt off. The neighbors were completely assuming that they were having sex in the condo, and, well, it seemed to go against the good of what actually was taking place inside."

"You are right on. I find it interesting how I hear so many saying that men and women should never be alone, and they should never talk about personal matters with one another. Although it is good to be wise about how much detail one gives to the opposite sex, because, face it, there is information that should not be shared, but the Father delights when His daughters learn to trust His sons, and vice versa."

"So then what was the off feeling about, Holy Spirit?"

"The off feeling stems from them being alone. Being alone isn't wrong, but it's the time and the location that was wrong. You see, they opened the door for non-believers to slander their character, and it will be so much harder now for Taemin to bring those neighbors to the Father, because although he says he is a believer they see him as a normal man of the world. It would have been better for them to go during the day or early night at a public location. Although being alone is fine, it shouldn't be in a place that will allow room for their characters to be questioned. So instead they could have gone for coffee, dinner/lunch/breakfast, they could have met at the mall. The point is that although alone, they would still be in a public place. But if that was the only time and place available, then they should have had another woman be there with them or an older couple who could also be there to keep those in the world from misunderstanding the situation. Because remember, they are the ones we want to reach for the Father."

"That makes sense. I'm beginning to understand that we need each other. I was reading my Bible yesterday and I came across 1 Timothy 5:1-2 (NIV) which says, '[1] Do not rebuke an older man harshly, but exhort him as if he were your father. Treat younger men as brothers, [2] older women as mothers, and younger women as sisters, with absolute purity.' How I treat my brothers should be done in purity and same for them, they should treat me with purity. I also have heard it said that women shouldn't share personal stuff with men and vice versa, but I got to thinking about the days and times we are living in. Holy Spirit, I am living in dark days, where the church throughout the world is being targeted, or at least starting to be. One day we will see the fulfillment of Revelations. We need to know who of our brothers we can trust, because in those days we will be like the underground church in Rome. We need to know who we can trust, who has our backs, who is filled with the Father's wisdom, and we need to know how to communicate with one another. If we don't start now, what are we going to do when those times come? We need each other like never before."

"Well said, Aubrey. It sounds like the Father is bringing understanding to you even now. Now I want to take you on a journey to see brother and sisters who are doing things right. Are you ready?"

"Am I ready? Of course I'm ready to see some good things happen, because my heart was hurting like crazy through this last journey."

"Mine too, Aubrey. In fact, the Father's heart, the Son's heart, and My heart were all hurting. Come, let's get on with our journey."

"Alright, let's go."

Chapter 7

Swiftly I was Philip-Transported, and as I straightened out my dress I looked around in surprise, "Ummm...Holy Spirit, weren't we here before? Isn't...isn't this the Chinese restaurant where David experienced his greatest hurt?"

"Good job, you remembered. This is in fact the same restaurant. Remember how I told you I wanted to wait to discuss what you observed about David and Becca?"

"I remember. Is it time now to talk about it?"

"Yes, but instead of you sharing your observations with Me, I want you to ask Me the questions you were contemplating on your walk in the park."

"Okay. My heart really ached for David, but I also understood Becca's response. In fact, through the years I have heard many women say that, and I began to wonder how this situation should have been handled. It's not like we can keep changing ourselves to please everyone, but at the same time, are there some things that we are to let go of for the best of others?"

"That is an excellent question. Before I answer, I want to tell you what happened to David after we left him."

I nodded, a bit concerned. The Holy Spirit sounded so serious, and I felt a sadness to His voice.

"David went home after leaving the restaurant. He was hurting inside and felt confused and ashamed that he was still struggling to overcome porn, lust, and pleasuring himself. And he felt abandoned. His sister had sat across from him and judged him, even going so far as to be angry and resentful over being asked to help. Depression soon set in, but nothing could have prepared David for what Becca would do next.

"Instead of being obedient to Proverbs 17:9 (NIV) which says, '⁹ Whoever would foster love covers over an offense, but whoever repeats the matter separates close friends.' Becca went and told a couple of her close friends about David asking her to change how she dressed. The very idea of changing herself for anyone caused all the girls to talk badly about David. Except Becca had no idea the consequences of this. The girls she had told went and told the other girls in the youth group, who went and told the boys in the youth group as well. Soon, everyone in the church knew that David had a sin problem with porn, lust, and pleasuring himself. The whole church turned on David. People talked about him behind his back, but then they started talking about him in front of him. They judged him and told him how sinful he was, completely ignoring the fact that he was getting help for it.

"Not only did the church turn on David, but they began to judge his mother and view his younger sister differently. In an instant, David lost his church family. He felt it was his fault his family was unfairly judged, and he lost his second dad as well. Remember how I told you that Becca's dad had taken over the role of a father after David's own father passed away?"

"I remember. What happened to David?"

"I wish I could say it got better quickly, but it didn't. David spiraled into a dark depression and one month later he attempted suicide."

I gasped in horror not knowing what to say. I had been there before. I had been to that dark depression, and had planned out my own death. By the grace of the Father, and through the audible voice of the Holy Spirit I was saved. I didn't know what to say, but I knew the Holy Spirit understood what I was feeling.

"I know, you have been there too, child. David's suicide wasn't successful though. The gun he used misfired, stopped by an angel on the scene. At the very moment it misfired, David received a call from his youth pastor. The youth pastor had stuck by his side throughout the ordeal. He expressed how the church's response to David was wrong, and when he confronted them they didn't repent and change, so he had decided to take a job at a different church and invited David and his family to join him there.

"David's heart broke at that moment and he told the youth pastor everything that had just happened. The youth pastor rushed to where David was sitting in his car, took the gun, and held David like a father holds a son. From that day on, he became a father to David. Slowly, David and his family began to heal and they were able to forgive Becca and their old church.

"But sadly, Becca forever lost the brother relationship she had with David. Eventually her family found out her role in the matter and although they made things right with David and his family, the relationship had been altered and could never go back to what it once was. In fact, the Father in His love chose to let David and his family start over with new family and friends."

"I feel bad that Becca missed out on her brother and sister relationship with David, and I am thankful that David was able to find a family, but I'm wondering how this answers my question."

The Holy Spirit chuckled, "I knew you were going to ask that. In order to answer that question, let's observe David now."

My eyes widened in shock at the Holy Spirit's words. I have to admit I got super excited to know that I would observe David again. I hoped that what I would see would show that he had overcome his sin.

"Do you see him?"

I strained to see and then straightened up in surprise. David was sitting just one table away, and I almost didn't recognize him. It was obvious he was older, probably in his junior year of college. Sitting next to him was a beautiful girl. I began to observe.

David looked much like he did when he was younger, but there was a maturity to him and his features were a bit more accentuated. He had on a pair of shorts and t-shirt that had John 3:16, his favorite verse, on it. He smiled at Rebecca, the girl sitting across from him. They had been friends for a year now. She moved to town to go to the same college he went to, and they had actually met at church first. After getting to know each other, David had shared his past experience at another church with her. She was moved with compassion for him. David had grown a lot during these years. He had found victory over porn, lust, and pleasuring himself, and the Father had shown him what habits to implement in his life for continued freedom.

Rebecca was full of life and joy and kindness. She had dark brown eyes, brown curly hair, and round cheeks. She had come to America from Europe for school, and was still adjusting to the culture. Tonight she was wearing a sleeveless black mini dress. She was beautiful, and turned heads in the restaurant.

David prayed before talking, asking the Father to give him the right words to use.

"Rebecca, I actually wanted to talk to you about something,

and I pray that you take this right way, and understand it's out of love."

Rebecca nodded, a bit apprehensive at how serious David was.

"So you know my story and what the Father helped me overcome, but that doesn't mean satan doesn't tempt me anymore. In fact, if I don't remain in the Father and keep following the habits He gave me, the temptation rushes in like a hurricane. Lately, I have noticed that he has been tempting me more in my thoughts of you. I know part of it is your culture, but you are definitely a hands-on girl, and you naturally touch those around you when you are talking. However, I struggle with it, especially because of what you wear when you are doing it. I'm not judging you, or asking you to change, because I know it's my problem. So with that being said, I need some distance from you until I am able to overcome these thoughts towards you. I want to honor you and protect you as my sister. I hope you understand my heart."

David waited quietly for Rebecca's response, his heart racing in fear. He was taking a leap of faith repeating the same situation that he had with Becca, even at the same restaurant. Taking a deep breath, he prayed while he waited.

Rebecca had tears in her eyes when she finally responded. "Please don't apologize. I had no idea that what I was wearing and how I use my body was affecting you. I truly do not want to be a stumbling block in your relationship with God. But please, David, please don't stay away from me? Please give me the opportunity to change. From now on I will watch what I wear and make sure it isn't revealing or seductive. If I forget about my body language, please grace me and remind me? Maybe you could even give me a code word so I remember I need to be watchful of myself. Please give me a chance to change, because I really need you in my life. You have been a brother I never knew I was missing, and I know that the Father has a special plan for us, and I don't want to miss out on that."

David sat humbled, and with tears streaming down his face, he nodded. "Thank you, thank you for wanting me to still be a part of your life. I am willing to try if you are." He choked out the words as a smile spread across his face.

Rebecca smiled back at him. "I am willing. I am definitely willing."

And just like that, I was Philip-Transported outside a movie theater.

"What did you observe, Aubrey?" The Holy Spirit didn't give me any time to look at my surroundings.

I smiled through my tears at what I just witnessed. "It's like what John 15:12-15 (NIV) says, '12 My command is this: Love each other as I have loved you. 13 Greater love has no one than this: to lay down one's life for one's friends. 14 You are my friends if you do what I command. 15 I no longer call you servants, because a servant does not know his master's business. Instead, I have called you friends, for everything that I learned from my Father I have made known to you.' I always thought that this verse represented our actual life, our very breath. I always wondered how many individuals actually are given the opportunity to die for their friend, but at this moment I'm realizing there is an important detail I have missed in these verses. The Father is asking us to lay down our lives, the way we want to live, what we want to wear, how we want to speak and act, and the list goes on and on. He is telling us that a true friend, and a true child of God would be willing to lay those down for our brother or sister."

"Very good. You got the answer to the question you asked about changing for others. Love gives to others. It requires we lay down our own wants and desires for the better of the one we are loving. It sacrifices our flesh, and makes us walk in the spirit.

Becca chose her flesh, she chose her own desires and wants, missing out on God's plan for her. You see women in the church today who no longer care about how they represent God with their clothing. Sometimes you might not even be able to tell a difference based on appearance alone. But God longs for His daughters to be clothed in purity and honor. In fact, Rebecca will implement an amazing wardrobe change that actually compliments who she is on the inside. The colors and patterns are still beautiful and amazing, but they aren't revealing. Her body will no longer be the focal point, but Jesus, who lives inside of her, will be.

"I also want to make note here, Aubrey, that women are not the only ones who need to change. There are many men who are too physical with women. Although most mean nothing by it, (although some do), it can have the same effect on women. Women are visual too, and so it's important that men dress in a way that is honoring as well.

"Now there will be many who will have a problem with this, but Aubrey, do you remember what happened when you went to a Muslim country to teach and what they thought of you?"

"Do I remember? Of course I remember. They judged me immediately based off of what is in our movies, tv shows, and music. It took a month for them to see that I was not like what they thought an American was. One month to earn their respect. However, at the end of my time there, my students commented how they saw me as a white 'one of their own' in a sea of brown, that they respected me and acknowledged that my relationship with the Father was special. I tried to explain that to some of the girls when I got back, but they didn't understand how what they wear mattered. In the Western world, the clothing has become very scandalous. And there are many other countries that have followed suit. But there are even more countries where this is not normal or acceptable behavior. It brings judgements about the character of those who dress like that.

"As daughters of the King who are His ambassadors, we should be very aware of the clothing we wear. We should be living a lifestyle of purity and holiness that would draw people from other countries to God. Our appearance does matter, it affects how we are perceived and received. As the daughter of the King, I long to see many saved and none lost to the gates of Hell, so I will choose to present myself in honor, in purity, and in holiness, so the glory of God is revealed and not my body."

"You are right, Aubrey. Many women do not understand this concept, and many men do not understand that how they treat women, what they wear, and how they represent themselves also greatly affects how people in other countries view them.

"There is something else I want to point out to you, Aubrey. Becca chose not to obey the Father. She chose her flesh and what she wanted over what was holy and pure. Her choice altered the plan God had for her and David as brother and sister. He had a beautiful ministry that they were going to work in together. They would each get married to other people and Becca's husband and David's wife would also join in ministering together. Their children would grow up together in a loving environment. Although Becca forfeited her role, God's plan was still going full stream ahead. He just chose to bring in a girl who would honor Him and say yes to Him. Rebecca would now take Becca's place. The ministry to come will play a great role in the end time harvest."

"I didn't even think about that, Holy Spirit. You are right though. It makes me think of my ex-husband and I. He chose to have affairs, to abuse me, and to stop me from ministry. Ultimately his consequence was that he lost me and I am no longer in his life, nor does he have a role in the ministry the Father has given me. Instead, the Father has given that role to another."

"Exactly! Well, are you ready for the next observation?"

"Actually, I am. I feel like I am beginning to understand the important role You have called us into."

Chapter 8

"I thought you said it was time to observe, Holy Spirit?" I was super confused. I wasn't being Philip-Transported anywhere.

"I already Philip-Transported you from the condo to the movie theater. Your next observation takes place here."

"Ohhhhh." I suddenly noticed my surroundings in greater detail. I was standing outside a movie theater, and a chilly wind cooled my face and pulled at my dress. There was a line for a new Christian movie coming out for Christmas. Although the line wasn't extravagant, it was nice to see a line for a godly movie. I always saw longer lines for the worldly movies.

As I watched the line my eyes were drawn to a group of women in their early thirties. I looked around waiting for a man to approach them, but none appeared.

"Ummm...Holy Spirit, I feel Your nudge to watch these women, but where is the brother?"

I could hear the laughter in the Holy Spirit's voice when He answered me. "Observe, you will understand."

I nodded in confusion, but obeyed.

There were four women grouped together. Each were completely different from each other. Nicole was as Caucasian as one could get, with blonde hair and blue eyes and pale skin that looked like she just stepped out of the house for the first time in years. Her mid-western accent was in contradiction to Maria's Hispanic accent, Dan-Bi's South Korean accent, and Durra's Kenyan accent. Maria had beautiful black curly hair, thick as can be, dark brown eyes, and bronze skin. Dan-Bi on the other hand had medium brown eyes, a fair beige glow, and wavy black locks. Durra had beautiful rich black skin, black afro-textured hair, and deep brown eyes.

All four women came from different countries, with cultures and languages that, for some, could have been a hindrance in communication. But these four friends had met at a mission's school. Their love for God gave them a grace to take time to understand and treasure the differences between all four of them, and also enjoy the things they had in common. It had allowed them to form a close sisterhood, and they relied on each other for support and encouragement.

I moved closer to hear their conversation.

"Okay, so you know how we were just talking about how close we are with our brothers in Christ? I mean, we have served in foreign lands together and learned to rely on one another, which is not really something you see in the American church. This community that we have with one another and the way we have to rely on one another is different." Nicole voiced her thoughts as the other three friends listened to her. As she spoke, her thoughts grew deeper, because in that moment the Holy Spirit deposited truth to her spirit.

"So we talked about how although we are super close to our brothers in Christ, there are still some differences between what I would share with them, and what I would share with my blood brother."

Dan-Bi nodded. "I remember this conversation. We talked about how if it had to do with personal womanly stuff like periods, sex, or certain parts of our bodies, maybe even certain areas of our emotions."

"Exactly. So I have a story I wanted to share because we just had this conversation. So when it happened I was laughing to myself going, 'of course this would happen of all days.'" Dan-Bi, Durra, and Maria's interest was piqued.

"So yesterday I was hanging out with my brother Phil and my brother-in-Christ Peter. We decided to go Peter's house to watch a movie. During the movie, my stomach started hurting and when I went to the bathroom I found that my time had arrived early. So I started texting my brother and after ten minutes with no response it dawned on me that my brother had forgotten his phone at home. So I was left with a decision. I was so uncomfortable and wasn't sure how I should ask Peter for pads and a pair of shorts to wear. I was so embarrassed. All I remember was crying out, 'Um…Holy Spirit, what do I do?' and then it finally hit me that I could ask him to send my brother to the bathroom." All the girls started giggling at this.

"I can't imagine how awkward that must have been." Maria shook her head in mortification on Nicole's behalf.

"So what happened next, what did you say to Peter?" Durra asked.

"Well, I sent him a text saying, 'hey, ummm…I'm not feeling the greatest could you send my brother to the bathroom? I forgot he left his phone at home.' He texted back right away and said, 'Sure.' Pretty soon Phil showed up. I explained the situation and he quickly went to the car to get my pads out of my purse. When he got back inside he asked Peter if I could borrow some shorts because I had gotten them wet by accident. And just like that the situation was resolved without it being embarrassing for anyone."

"I love that you figured out a solution. I know that there are times when we have to be vulnerable with our brothers-in-Christ because there are no other options, and I think they want to be able to help. But when we have other options, I think it is wise to respect that relationship." Dan-Bi expressed a situation in school when she couldn't ask a girl or her brother for help, and had to ask her best friend who happened to be a male. "He helped me, but it definitely wasn't comfortable. I think it's good having a healthy understanding of what you should share with a blood brother, a brother-in-Christ, and then a husband, because each has a different role in our lives. Sometimes it's just following the Holy Spirit's leading on topics too, because you never know what things could be triggering to them, or vice versa, there could be things they shouldn't share with us, because of our own history and past."

"It's so true though, I think that women in the western world have kind of gotten comfortable with sharing personal information with the opposite sex, and I really recognized it after returning from the mission field. Like it really took me by surprise, because it's like there is no veil over their tongue anymore. It was actually a bit disappointing to see," Nicole said sadly.

"I think that is why the Father is asking us to make a new mold with the brothers-in-Christ here in America. It's to show them what a healthy relationship with a sister-in-Christ should be. They don't need us to vomit words all over them, and we should be more mindful of how what we share affects our relationships," Durra added.

I found myself nodding along with their conversation. There was such wisdom and love in what they were saying. It seemed like American women had allowed their tongues to loosen and I had to agree that there were times when I had done the same and it wasn't honoring to the brothers-in-Christ that were with me.

I felt the Holy Spirit's nudge to move on and as I walked away, pondering what I had heard, a deep cry pulled from my heart. "Holy Spirit, would you please help me have more control over my tongue? I want to honor my brothers-in-Christ, and even my sisters-in-Christ would benefit from this. If I fail to sense Your nudge, then I ask that You would convict me, so I would recognize what needs to be changed."

"Of course, Aubrey. I will help you guard your tongue."

I smiled and continued to follow His leading.

Chapter 9

As I made my way from the movie theater to the parking lot, I saw a man in his forties talking to a woman who appeared to be in her younger thirties. I watched, and after feeling the nudge, I made my way closer.

Alex was rugged in appearance. He had an earthy feel about him. Maybe it was the cowboy boots, cowboy hat, and flannel shirt that gave him that. He wore a leather winter coat too. His skin had a leathered look from being out in the sun for long hours every day in all sorts of weather conditions, and his green eyes held a hint of caution.

Angela, on the other hand, wore a jean skirt and flannel shirt with her cowgirl boots and a winter coat. She had her hair up in the braid and her hazel eyes glowed with the joys of a newfound love interest.

Alex was contemplating the best way of approaching the topic of Angela's new love interest. He had some concerns about the guy. There was something in the way that he treated Angela that gave him some red flags.

"Angela, did I ever share with you about my ex-wife?"

Angela paused to think about Alex's question. "You know, I think we have talked about her before, but not in great detail or anything. Is there something specific about her that's on your mind?"

Alex nodded and quietly prayed in his heart, "Holy Spirit, lead me, give me the right words, please."

"I met my ex-wife, Jen, when I was in my early twenties. She was a breath of fresh air. She was so beautiful and down to earth. She had a natural beauty that captivated every man that looked at her. She had it all, the looks, the attitude, the job, I mean she fit my list of what I was looking for down to a T." Alex laughed at his past inability to see Jen clearly.

"But there was something that I didn't see about her, or maybe I did but I was so attracted to her and I really wanted her to be the one, you know?"

Angela nodded her head in understanding.

"Well, it started when we had been dating for half a year. She would start pointing out my negative flaws, and in the same breath say how she did things right. At first, I thought maybe I wasn't giving her enough security and so she felt like she needed to put me down to feel better about herself. I even went so far as to question if I was saying things that made her feel like I was judging her in a negative way. I thought that as time went on she would understand my love for her and begin to see how I really saw her." Alex shook his head sadly.

"So I decided not to ask anyone for their thoughts and made up my mind to marry the gal. And marry we did. We had only been dating for seven months, were engaged for five months, and after only a year of being together we tied the knot. But Angela, nothing prepared me for what was about to come."

Angela listened closely, understanding that Alex was opening up about a place that had been painful.

"What I thought was just because I wasn't making her feel secure, turned out to be a complete joke. Instead, she became more and more negative about everything I did. Pretty soon she would blame me for her own mistakes too. I began to understand that it didn't have to do with security, but with her character. She thought she was good and could do no wrong, and everything was placed on my head. I tried to make the marriage work. We spent three miserable years together and by the end of it, I was so hurt and depleted of honor, and wondering if I was truly as bad as she claimed I was.

"It didn't take long for her to have an affair. I decided the marriage wasn't worth saving and we got divorced. I ended up having to go to a Christian counselor for a good year before I could really move on from that relationship."

Alex looked at Angela to see how she was receiving what he was sharing. After getting a nod of sympathy, Alex continued on. "I have been contemplating sharing my story for a couple of weeks now with you, but felt I needed to pray and see if the Lord wanted me to. You see, a couple weeks ago I was observing your guy friend and how he was communicating with you. I have to be honest, Angela, I noticed some red flags. I felt like I was hearing my ex-wife all over again."

Angela looked at Alex in surprise. "Really? I....guess I didn't notice that."

"Yeah, I could tell it kind of went over your head. I know you are really interested in this guy, and I know that you are attracted to both his look and attitude. But I want to encourage you to take time to observe his character, and see if it really lines up to the man you are wanting to spend your life with. I would also encourage you to talk to your parents. You have amazing parents who want the best for you and they are praying folk. I really wish that I had gotten my parents' advice and wisdom, because my uncle had actually told my dad he had seen some warning signs and so my parents were praying that I would receive some advice from them. But I refused."

Angela was quiet. She understood that Alex was wanting what was best for her. He could have kept his past experience to himself, but she knew that he was wanting her to escape the same experience he had.

"Thank you for sharing your story with me, Alex. I understand that you are sharing this with me because you don't want me to make the same mistake. You are right, I am really attracted to him, but I don't want to marry someone who will hurt me either. I will do as you said and take some time to watch his character. Later this week I am meeting my parents for lunch and I will ask them if they have observed anything, and if they haven't, I'll ask them to pray and observe as well. Thank you for being vulnerable with me."

Alex smiled. "Thank you for being willing to receive my counsel. I know it would be really easy to ignore my warning and turn a blind ear to what I said. I really appreciate your character and that you are being wise in your relationships."

Angela smiled back. "I am the one who's thankful to have a brother-in-Christ looking out for me. I have been praying for God to speak to me on this, and I need to be open and willing to hear answers that contradict my own feelings and desires. I want the truth, not lies."

Alex nodded. "I'm proud of you. I better get going. I'll see you at church on Sunday. Bye, Angela."

"Good-bye!"

I watched as both walked to their cars and drove off. I thought about my own relationship and how I wish I would have listened to the wise counsel my Father had put around me. But I didn't, I pushed through with my own agenda and suffered the consequences. After ten years of abuse, trauma, and his affairs, the divorce was a welcome relief. The healing process was so very needed, especially to learn new healthy habits to overcome the post-traumatic stress disorder. However, I also began to understand why the Father was having me share my story with others. He wanted to use me to warn others not to make the same mistake. He wanted to use my life to help others receive healing and freedom.

I looked around and noticed that while I had been absorbed in my thoughts, the Holy Spirit had Philip-Transported me to a coffee shop, and sitting in front of me was none other than Aaron and Ariella. "Um...Holy Spirit, why are they back?"

Chapter 10

This time I knew that the Holy Spirit was laughing at my reaction. I waited patiently—okay, I tried to wait patiently for His response.

"So I have a very good reason to bring them back. I showed you then that Aaron, Abraham, and Andrew each had an amazing brother and sister relationship with Ariella. However, Kanoa kind of fazed out the good by revealing the bad. So I wanted us to come back to their brother and sister relationship so you could see the way they function and their role with Ariella."

"That makes sense, and You are right. When I think back to that time, I really only remember my bad feelings from witnessing Kanoa's actions. I love the idea of redeeming my perspective of the rest of their relationships."

I turned to observe Aaron and Ariella.

The Steamy Brew was a local favorite coffee house. They worked hard to create unique blends and serve the best quality of coffee beans. The interior design of the coffee shop was unique as well. The walls were covered with artwork created by women and kids who had been saved from human trafficking. The artwork was for sale and one hundred percent of the money earned from each sale would go back to the women and children. They also gave their monthly tips to a nonprofit organization that helped victims of human trafficking as well.

The furniture was locally made, which was a great way for the locals to gain recognition and sales. The coffee store was lively and vibrant, and there was always a steady flow of traffic coming through.

Ariella and Aaron were sitting farthest away from the main doors, close to where a brick fireplace was located. Here it was cozy and not as overwhelming for the senses.

"How have you been doing lately, Ariella?"

Ariella thought for a bit. It had been a month since she and Kanoa parted ways after that horrible experience. It still left a bad taste in her mouth, and to have to still see him at work had also given her a lot to think about concerning her future.

"Honestly, I feel extremely embarrassed and humiliated when I think about that day. I really didn't handle myself well. I'm embarrassed that I cried, and that so many people witnessed my meltdown at the restaurant. I…I don't know what to feel and think about it anymore."

Aaron nodded in understanding. "I kind of gathered that after we all sat down and talked about the whole experience later that week. I was super frustrated and upset with Kanoa for treating you that way and causing you such pain and hurt. I know that it was a hard decision for you to tell him you couldn't hang out anymore, but it truly was a wise move."

"I know you are right, it was what I was supposed to do. The idea of talking to him after it all happened terrified me, and I have no words to express how amazing it was when Andrew told me that he would talk to Kanoa in my place and that I just needed to be a body present."

Aaron smiled. "He sure is a good brother. I know the three of us sat down and talked about which one of us should be the one to talk to him, and I was honest with them. I told them that my anger towards Kanoa would make the situation backfire and that one of them who had a better heart towards him at that moment should go with you. Now that it's been a month, I've been able to let go of my anger and resentment towards him. But I wanted to talk with you, because I can tell you're still struggling with something from it."

"You're right, I am. Through all these years you have been encouraging me and helping me learn habits to overcome my sensory overload in a way that honored God. Instead of having meltdowns and closing down, I learned how to pull myself away for a bit and rest in God and then come back and enjoy the rest of whatever I was doing. I have learned how to express when I need alone time, or when I need to be around others and not feel judged about it. I've incorporated so many habits, even down to a weighted blanket at night. But that day I realized I still have my bad days where I make mistakes and I don't handle it well. I also worried that it was because I didn't explain it correctly to Kanoa."

"I think you have a lot of fears, and you are taking a lot of responsibility of that day upon yourself. There were two of you present and both of you had a part to play in the events that took place. It's true that we brothers have worked hard to create a safe place for you where you could learn and grow, make mistakes and change, without being judged and hurt. But not everyone is like that. Not everyone creates a place for friends to be their real, flawed self without being embarrassed, fearful or living in doubts. We chose to be that for you, though. We wanted you to have the freedom to be yourself, to watch you come out of your shell, and at the same time encourage you towards becoming even more like Jesus. I know that this is something we have talked about before, but I want to remind you, part of what you are struggling with is that you no longer want to let anxiety and sensory overload keep you from being obedient to God, and that also goes with how you respond to those situations. So let's go back to that day. Okay?"

Ariella nodded. She knew that she needed to face that day to overcome the fear it brought, and she knew she needed God's help. *Father, help me.* "Okay, let's do it."

Aaron smiled with pride, knowing this was a big step for Ariella. "So that day, you did make some mistakes. Some of your responses and attitude towards him were not Christlike, especially at the apartment after he had hurt you. I think it's important you own that part, repent, and allow the Holy Spirit to cleanse you. Then ask Him to help you walk in spirit, not in flesh. The other thing is that you need to forgive and release Kanoa for what he did to you. The words and attitude were not of Christ and they were wrong, but holding on to them has no affect on him, it's you who's held hostage by it now. You need to release him and forgive. Let God work in his life and bring justice to you."

"You are right. I haven't been willing to forgive him or myself. I have been held hostage by it, and I haven't been able to move on from that night. It's gotten to the point that I hate going to work and seeing him. I have even prayed about if I'm supposed to find a different job."

"I can see how that would definitely be the easy way out, but the Father might be asking you to stay and reveal Christ to him and the others at your workplace. "

"That's what I'm scared of. Because if He tells me to stay, I know that I cannot disobey, and yet I really want the easy way out."

"I think there are times when most of us want the easy way out, but we have to remember that God has a calling on our lives, and when we agree to live for Him, that means we take the hard way."

Ariella was convicted; she knew Aaron was right. The Holy Spirit was confirming it in her spirit. "You are right. I'm not supposed to take the easy way out. I am supposed to show Christ to them. I will really need you guys to pray for me though, because it won't be easy. I know I need to do it, but I need your prayer support."

"You have it, we are always praying for you and we will continue to pray for you. We want God's best for you and we want to see you reach your full potential and work in the opposite of anxiety and sensory overload. We want to see Christ triumphant and the demonic spirits defeated."

Ariella smiled, a look of peace shining on her face. In that moment, she knew she could face this giant.

Wow! Tears began to flow from my eyes witnessing this beautiful brother and sister moment. It was so full of the Father's presence that when the Holy Spirit Philip-Transported me to the bottom of a mountain I wasn't exactly happy.

Chapter 11

It took me a minute to change my attitude about being Philip-Transported away from Aaron and Ariella. But I also knew the Holy Spirit did it for a reason and I needed to get my attitude in alignment so I could hear and see clearly.

I took a deep breath and asked for forgiveness for my anger at being interrupted. "Holy Spirit, I'm sorry. I know You have a reason to interrupt what I am doing, and my anger towards You is not right. I ask You over and over to interrupt my day and let Your will be known, and then when You do it I don't have the right attitude. Please forgive me. I'm choosing to change my attitude and get into alignment with You."

"I forgive you, Aubrey. I know it's hard to surrender the assumed control, but I love seeing how your heart is so quick to move with Me. You are right, I needed to get you here quickly so you didn't miss this next beautiful moment. Are you ready?"

"Yes, I am ready. I have adjusted myself and You are right, I don't want to miss the beautiful moment with You."

I turned at the sound of a jeep approaching and watched a man and woman get out. They had such an outdoorsy look to them.

Steve and Samantha had been friends for a couple of years now. They met at a gym and soon learned that they were both believers. Samantha had just recently moved to town and was looking for a church so it made sense for Steve to invite her to his. Soon she was included in his friend group at church and they all began to connect and grow as believers in Christ. Samantha had just turned thirty and her biggest struggle was the desire for a relationship. But it seemed like God was telling her to wait on it. Every guy she had met seemed as if he wasn't interested in her, including Steve.

In fact, a year into being friends she had shared with Steve how she had begun to admire him and her feelings had started to change from brother and sister into wanting something more. Steve, however, didn't feel the same.

Samantha had short blonde hair, hazel eyes, and bronze skin. She loved being out in nature and hiking was her favorite activity. Because of her love for anything active, she had a very toned body. In other people's eyes she had amazing looks, and her personality was God-fearing and loving. Yet, it seemed like she was constantly waiting for the right one.

Steve was tall and lanky, blue-eyed with curly brown hair that he wore a bit longer than most guys do, and although he enjoyed the outdoors, sports wasn't his thing. However, he'd really been wanting to go on this hike. A lot of his friends had been talking about how amazing this hike was and how the views could only have been created by God. When he thought about who he wanted to go with, Samantha had come to mind. She loved the outdoors and being active, and she had been here before, so she could keep them from getting lost.

"Are you ready, Samantha? I brought my camera along like you said to. Make sure you let me know all the best places for pictures."

"Sounds good, I will definitely let you know. Let's get our backpacks and water and head out."

I followed silently behind them, trying not to be captivated by the views and reminding myself I was here to observe the individuals and not my Father's handiwork. Maybe the Holy Spirit would let me look another time.

"Wow! Samantha, look over there! I see two deer." Steve could not hold back his burst of excitement. Thankfully the deer were far enough away they didn't hear him.

Samantha stopped to observe the deer. She and Steve were probably thirty feet up the mountain, and between the pine trees was a view of a wide valley. Down below a mother deer and her baby fawn were making their way to the river. Samantha had to agree, the view was breathtaking. The sky was clear and only a few puffy white clouds drifted by.

They continued their way up the mountain, taking a couple minutes for rest and water breaks. The scenery was spectacular and Samantha paused to praise God for His amazing handiwork and for the closeness she felt to Him in this moment.

Midway up the mountain Samantha paused and looked at her watch. "I think we should stop here. The sun is about to start setting and if we go further up it will be too dark on the way back down."

"Oh good thinking. I didn't think of that when I set the time up for this hike. I should have considered that."

"No problem. Do you want to take a few more pictures and then we will head back down?"

"Sure...um...actually, could we stay for the sunset and then just quick make our way down? I do have my phone totally charged if we need a flashlight for the last bit."

Samantha struggled inwardly for a moment, but didn't feel like she could say no. "Sure, that's fine."

They made their way over to a large rock to sit and watch the sun set. As they were watching, Samantha knew she needed to say something. 'Holy Spirit, please give me the right words and let him not take offense,' she prayed silently, bolstering her courage.

"Steve, could I talk to you about something?"

"Sure, what's up?"

"I want to thank you for thinking of me for this hike, but I have to be honest with you, I won't be able to go on any more hikes with you."

Steve looked at Samantha in surprise. "Why?"

"The Lord has made me to love nature, to be close to Him when I am in nature. To me, hiking in the mountains is a very intimate experience. So with that in mind, it makes sense that when I'm in nature, the setting feels romantic to me. There is something about it that stirs my heart. I know that not every girl is the same. Some would be here and think I'm crazy to call this romantic, but that's how God made me. His creation, His nature, is the place where I feel the stirring of romance and the budding of feelings. You and I have talked about my feelings before. I know that you will not ever be returning my affection for you. I have been taking these last couple of months to work through my feelings for you and let you go. So I have to be honest with you, being here in this setting is not helping me. It's not healthy for me to be here with you in this place. It's not honoring to you either, because I know where your heart is at."

Steve looked out at the sunset, deeply convicted. "You're right. I wasn't thinking about you and your feelings when I asked you to go hiking with me. To me this is just hike, it's just nature, and although I admire what God has created it doesn't have the same impact on me that it does on you. I'm so sorry, Samantha. I wasn't being considerate to your feelings and heart, and I kind of just ignored what you must be feeling and was only concerned about what I wanted. Please forgive me? I wasn't being a respectful brother to you."

Samantha smiled sadly. "I forgive you, and I'm sorry too. I had sensed a red flag in my spirit from the Holy Spirit, telling me this wasn't something I should do with you. It would cause my heart and mind to long for you, and I should have listened to Him. Please forgive me?"

Steve returned the smile. "I forgive you. I guess this is a learning experience to understand that I need to be more aware of all my sisters and what activities affect them differently. If I don't have feelings for them, I need to be careful not to put them in situations that would affect their heart if I am not willing to take responsibility for them."

"I like that. I think it's wise for men to be aware that if they are coming across as more intimate than just a brother, they really need to allow the Holy Spirit to lead them in how to be brother, so they don't use their sister and run from the responsibility of awakening their heart. The same goes for us women. If we know that our brother's heart is not leading towards a relationship, then we need to be aware of which activities are honoring for our brother and which aren't."

"I like that, Samantha. It shows that both brothers and sisters have a responsibility to protect one another's hearts and do what is best for the other. For me, I assumed you would have no problem going on this hike and I put my own heart first. I should have put your heart first and recognized the pain it would cause and found a different activity that we could do. I promise that, going forward, I will allow the Holy Spirit to lead me in our brother and sister relationship, and I will do my best not to put you in a situation where I awaken your heart."

"Thank you, Steve. I will also listen to the Holy Spirit in our brother and sister relationship. I will honor you as a brother and make sure I guard my heart, keeping you as just that."

I watched as Steve and Samantha made their way back down the mountain. I went and settled on the same rock they had been sitting on, and as I looked out over the valley, I rested. I knew that my journey through brother and sister relationships had ended, and that it was time for the Holy Spirit and I to talk through what I had seen, heard, and learned, and to discuss the blueprints the Father was wanting to reveal.

"But first, Aubrey, let's sit here and rest in each other's company."

"Okay, Holy Spirit."

Chapter 12

"Aubrey, before we begin to go deep, I want to take you to the top of the mountain."

I smiled in anticipation of the view.

"Okay, sounds good to me."

In an instance I was standing at the top of the mountain. The view was beyond what I could imagine. In front of me stretched the beautiful valley, with a stream running through it. Gorgeous trees spread throughout the wide expanse, everything lush and green. I turned around to see what view the other side of the mountain would bring, and my eyes widened in surprise. I could see mountain tops that sloped lower, but there were other mountains looming high above the one I stood on. I gazed up at them, surprised at how large they appeared from this distance.

"Holy Spirit, I was so focused on the view of the valley, I never looked at the view on the other side."

The Holy Spirit laughed gently. "It's okay. It is normal for humans to be so focused on what is in front of them that they forget to ask Me for the perspective that shifts their view. You chose to sit with Me, and you were willing to let Me bring you to the top of this mountain. I knew then that your eyes were open, so I could reveal even more of the details around you that you were missing."

"Thank you, Holy Spirit, for not giving up on me, and continuing to pursue my heart. I know that the Father's ways are not my own, and He knows and sees things that are beyond my imagination. Please remind me in the future when I forget to look through His eyes."

"Of course, it is the Father's heart for you to see through His eyes. He tells me over and over how to go about pursuing your heart and the best way to deliver information to you. He truly knows you best. Not only that, but Jesus, Yeshua, is standing before the Father and reminding Him to pursue you. He reminds Him of what you have done, where you need to go, and how your heart is His. With all three of Us actively going after you, the only one that would keep you from pursuing Us in return is yourself."

I nodded in understanding. "I don't want to block my relationship with You three. I want to be proactive in pursuing Your heart too and letting the world see what a relationship with the Trinity is all about. I want them to see the intimacy, that You are all focused on relationship, and that the Trinity is a personal God, fully desiring our hearts. I want the world to see what it looks like when a human responds to a relationship with You."

I could sense the joy my words brought the Father, and I could feel the Father's laughter spilling over me as His great love enveloped my heart.

"Aubrey, it's time that we talk about the journey of brother and sister relationship. We saw the things that are not of the Father. We witnessed how the children of God shunned one another, especially the ones who had repented and were working to change their habits and overcome their sin. We saw how children of God no longer guarded their hearts and allowed their tongues to speak crudeness and perversity, mocking the sacrifice of Yeshua (Jesus). Our hearts broke as we witnessed children of God forget that they are to encourage their brothers and sisters to reach their full potential and walk in their callings, but instead allowed satan to use them to destroy that which God had ordained. We saw how brothers and sisters chose not to allow their sibling in Christ to be themselves, nor encouraged them to grow more like Jesus. And finally, we also witnessed how deep conversations can be done in the wrong way.

"On the other hand, we witnessed brothers and sisters walking out 1 Thessalonians 5:11 (NIV) which says, '11 Therefore encourage one another and build each other up, just as in fact you are doing.' We saw the power of brotherly love found in Proverbs 17:9 (NIV), '9 Whoever would foster love covers over an offense, but whoever repeats the matter separates close friends.' We saw brothers and sisters correcting one another, and encouraging one another to obedience in Christ. Proverbs 27:5-6 (NIV) says, '5 Better is open rebuke than hidden love. 6 Wounds from a friend can be trusted, but an enemy multiplies kisses.' And not only did they respond well to the correction, but they also gave Me room to work in the situation and let Me lead them into all that Father had for them. We even witnessed Philippians 2:3-4 (NIV), which says, '3 Do nothing out of selfish ambition or vain conceit. Rather, in humility value others above yourselves, 4 not looking to your own interests but each of you to the interests of the others.'

"Aubrey, we witnessed such beautiful examples of brothers and sisters working together for the Father's kingdom."

"It's true. I have treasured seeing things through the Father's eyes. I sometimes forget that our very lives can be a hindrance to others coming to know the Father. My heart broke when His children cared more about their desires, their flesh, and their own way, instead of seeing how their lives were being used by satan to affect the kingdom of God. I also realized something extremely important: we need You to be an active part of our everyday lives. When we give You full control and allow You to interrupt our days, we get to experience life like we never imagined. I also understood that there is no totally-bulletproof plan that works with brother and sister relationships because we are all created differently, and we have all experienced different things in life that affect how we think and process life. For instance, how Samantha found nature romantic and Steve didn't. Which only shows us that we need You to be an active part in our relationships with others, so that we can keep our brother and sister relationships pure."

"It's true. I was sent to lead You all, to give direction and understanding, to bring to remembrance all that the Father wants you to remember, and yet, many in the church have chosen to shun Me. They ignore My existence, they force Me out of the church, and take away My freedom to interpret their Sundays. Many now say I am just a symbol of power, and yet I am here, I haven't left them. No, they have left Me. They live their lives shutting Me out. They ignore the conviction I bring, until it's finally so faint or nonexistent. And they wonder why life is so hard, why relationships are so hard, and why their love for God grows cold.

"Aubrey, the Father wants His bride, His remnant, to begin walking in a new wineskin. This begins with the very basics of walking with Me and allowing Me to be a part of every minute of every day. This first step will change everything when it comes to brother and sister relationships. I will be able to help each one navigate relationships and learn how to live pure with one another."

"Wow! I feel like for many this will be a very easy step, but just like You mentioned, too may churches teach that

You are not real, that You are just a symbol of power. So for many this will be a very hard and difficult step, because they will need to learn what the Bible actually says about You."

"Yes, they will need to renew their minds and perspectives of Who I am and the role the Father gave Me. Another step is one that the Father had you write about in Beyond Held Hostage, and that is the step of Tribe. When you look at the church and believers today, you don't see tribes. You see cliques, and you see everyone being about their own lives and business. They will spend time talking on Sunday and then ignore each other besides reaching out through social media throughout the week, maybe. But what happens when they are faced with sin, when their past is revealed, when their present is filled with suffering and they need support? What happens then? Does the tribe come together, or are they like ships sailing alone?"

"Hmmm...you are right. It wasn't until I wrote about Tribe and started hearing it mentioned in Spirit-filled churches that I realized this was a part of the Father's realignment He was carrying out."

"Correct, He is getting His bride back in realignment. So a good place for us to start is to talk about a Tribe and what that should look like."

"Okay, where do we begin?"

"When we think about Israel and the culture and how they lived, we begin to understand how very separated we have become in the church. In ancient times, tribes lived in cities together, and they were each given sections of land to live in. We find this information in Numbers 34, where it talks about the locations of Israel's borders, and in Joshua 13 we find that each tribe was given land to govern. Within each tribe there were family tribes, which had a nuclear household. Large families would live together or in close proximity, possibly with a courtyard separating them.[1]

"We find in Acts 2:44-47 (NIV) a better understanding of how the New Testament Tribe worked together. It says, '[44] All the believers were together and had everything in common. [45] They sold property and possessions to give to anyone who had need. [46] Every day they continued to meet together in the temple courts. They broke bread in their homes and ate together with glad and sincere hearts, [47] praising God and enjoying the favor of all the people. And the Lord added to their number daily those who were being saved.'

"So if we are to look at the Bride of Christ as a Tribe, we should see believers working together for His kingdom. They should be interacting with one another daily, meeting with one another, encouraging one another, coming alongside one another, and spending time with the Father together. They provided for each other, instead of expecting the government to do so. They would eat meals together and live life together. The underground church would help protect each other, and would pray for those who were suffering or about to be murdered for Yeshua.

"The Tribe will be a place where you will belong and have a place to safely heal, grow, learn, and be equipped to move out and take ground for the

---

[1] Biblical Archaeology Society Staff, "Daily Life in Ancient Israel". 2023. https://www.biblicalarchaeology.org/daily/ancient-cultures/ancient-israel/daily-life-in-ancient-israel/

Father. The Tribe will work together to bring the Kingdom of God to earth, and they will spread the Gospel throughout the world. The Tribe will not function like the church of old. I will be allowed in to disrupt the old ways and bring forth the will of the Father. My gifts, the Gifts of The Spirit, will be activated throughout the Tribe, and each member will begin to learn how to use them as weapons of warfare.

"The Tribe will become the warrior Bride of Christ. They will begin to function in authority and anointing, and they will charge the gates of Hades and bring deliverance to those in bondage. The Tribe is about to explode in favor, and the glory of God will be revealed through their lives. The ministries that will be birthed within Tribes will blow the minds of the church of Old, for the Tribe will begin to align their lives with the Word of God, and the Father's standard will be their standard. Culture, fear of man, popularity, and even the old church will no longer dictate how they live and walk. Instead, their walk will be blameless and they will study the Word, 'Bible' with fervency and allow Me to lead them into habits and lifestyles that will bring them before kings and rulers of nations. They will give an account of who the Father is, and many will lose their lives for Yeshua, but the power of the Father will only spread. The world and the old church will not be able to stop what the Father is about to do with His Tribe."

"Wow! I feel so honored that I get to be a part of this. So to understand the Tribe, its culture, its function, and how we live life together, basically means we know the Bible and live out the Bible. It means that we allow You to be active in our lives every day and follow Your leading, and say yes to the Father in whatever He asks us. Seems simple, and yet it's so contrary to the flesh that it truly has become all-out warfare."

"Yes, simple in word, but to actually apply it means dying to yourself, taking up your cross, and following Yeshua."

"I'm beginning to understand that the problem of the old church is that we make things so much harder than they are meant to be, and by allowing the culture of the world to influence us, we have become something we were never meant to be."

"You're right, which is why the Father is calling His Tribe into realignment and the new wineskin. I want you to do a study. I want you to look up the stats of sin taking place within the church and how many struggle with it."

"Okay, but I don't think I will like what I find.

"I found that according to a 2015 Lifeway Research study, 'Seven in 10 women who have had an abortion identify as a Christian.'[2] The main reasons are that the church is not equipped to handle this sin, the individual's own fear of shunning and condemnation, or just the plain truth that she will be alone on this journey because the church won't know how to walk out the needed healing in pregnancy outside of marriage.

"For porn addiction in men, a 2014 survey by Barna group showed that fifty percent of Christian men are addicted to

---

[2] Aaron Earls, "7 in 10 Women Who Have Had an Abortion Identify as a Christian." 2021. https://research.lifeway.com/2021/12/03/7-in-10-women-who-have-had-an-abortion-identify-as-a-christian/

porn.[3] It is also shown that women are also addicted to porn, and it is also a very strong contributor to divorce and affairs.

"It is hard to find statistics for masturbation, but if you research and look up what churches say or teach or believe about it...one can only assume that there is a very large amount of men and women who self-pleasure.

"When I researched affairs, I found it surprising how many pastors are actively having affairs, let alone how many husbands and wives are sinning too. No wonder the generations coming up believe that marriage is just a piece of paper and doesn't mean anything.

"I haven't even gotten into addictions, abuse, or even same-sex marriage and transgenderism within the old church. The truth is, the old church appears the same as the world. There is nothing separating them from the world. By kicking You out, by ignoring the Father's Word, 'Bible', and by refusing to live for Yeshua, the old church has become dead bones. Their appearance becomes less and less like the Father. No wonder God is calling His Tribe to realign, to set themselves apart from the world."

"You are right. Sin is rampant in the old church. Not only sin in action, but in thought, heart, and word. The old church no longer resembles a pure bride, and many have become deceived, calling, 'evil good and good evil'."

"I get it. What You are saying is that in order to have the right brother and sister relationship, we first need to have a

---

[3] John Thorington, "Porn in the Church-a Study." 2020. https://www.restoringheartscounseling.com/2020/12/21/is-porn-addiction-a-problem-in-your-church/

deep, committed covenant relationship with the Trinity. If we are fully pursuing the Father and walking out His Word, 'Bible,' then we and the relationships here on earth will function in spirit instead of in flesh."

"Exactly! That is the reason that Beyond Held Hostage had to be written before this book on relationships. Because without the right relationship with Us…satan will always sabotage relationships here on earth.

"Just think, Aubrey, how so many churches say, 'we accept you for who you are just like Jesus does.' And when people come, they are never told to die to flesh and walk in spirit. They are not told that what they are doing is sin and they need to realign themselves. Instead, the church is silent and the people remain in bondage to flesh. Yet, love is telling someone (in gentleness and kindness) that they are in sin and that the Father longs for them to come out of bondage, no longer hostages, but free the way He intended them to be.

"In Beyond Held Hostage, the Father also had you write about perspective. How you view your brothers and sisters will cause you to respond in either flesh or spirit. Many singles struggle with the right perspective of brother/sister because they are viewing them as a potential spouse instead. They forgot to look at them through the Father's eyes. Imagine how brother and sister relationships would change if we just saw each other as family the way the Father intended."

"Wow! I am beginning to understand the steps the Father has led me to in order to write this. So the first step, Holy Spirit, is that we begin to have a covenant relationship with the You, Yeshua, and the Father, walking out what the Bible says, and allowing You to be a part of our days.

"The second step is to take those truths and apply them to our relationships here on earth. We walk in step with You, following Your leading. We walk in love towards our brothers and sisters and keep our relationships pure and holy. We function in spirit together and stay away from flesh.

"When we apply both steps together, we will find ourselves walking in Tribe straight out of the book of Acts."

The Holy Spirit laughed again. "Exactly! It's so simple. Now the hard part begins. Not just to know it, but to act upon it."

"Holy Spirit, I know that there is so much to these blueprints that I can't even speak on it accurately, but I ask that You would reveal all these truths to the Tribe. That every single one of us would be given understanding in how to be a brother or a sister. That we would walk in obedience to what You show us. Holy Spirit, please continue to lead us in this relationship. Continue to open our eyes and ears to how the Father wants to take us deeper into understanding, wisdom, and knowledge in the area of brother and sister relationship. I ask this of You, in Jesus' name. So be it!"

"I will do all that you have asked, for your prayer is in alignment with the Father's heart. His answer is, 'Yes, and Amen!' He is proud of your prayer, Aubrey. He also sees that you are ready for the next part of the journey, that of relationship between those dating and those engaged."

Part 2

Dating/engaged Relationships

Chapter 13

"Aubrey, I have led you in observing those in brother and sister relationships because that is the very first area most individuals experience when it comes to relationships. But even though it's usually the first relationship within the family of God, the very first is your relationship with the Father. As we witnessed in part one of our journey, the relationship with the Father, with Yeshua, and with Me, the Holy Spirit, is the most important thing.

"No matter what kind of relationship you are in or what you are longing for, if you want it done right, it all starts in relationship with the Trinity. If it doesn't, nothing you do will give you the relationship your spirit longs for.

"As we stand on this mountaintop and look out over the Father's splendor, we have processed the first part of our journey. Our second leg of the journey begins now. I want you to make sure that you observe every detail. The old church has long forgotten the Father's intention with dating and engagements. Both areas have started to look more and more like the world. What I will have you observe will bring light to the darkness, shatter the lie of the enemy, and then bring in the realignment and blueprints the Father wants you to run with when it comes to dating and engagement. Are you ready, Aubrey?"

"I am ready, Holy Spirit. My emotions are a bit mixed up when it comes to this topic. I can see where fear wants to keep me from moving forward, the fear of past trauma happening again. But I understand that this is just another tactic the enemy would like to use to keep me held hostage.

But I refuse. I refuse to let him win the battle that Yeshua already won. So I have determined to go with You bravely. Lead the way, Holy Spirit."

As I looked out over the mountain range, I began to hear voices. I turned my eyes from the path I was on to see a young man and woman making their way up to the top.

"Justin, slow down, you are going too fast," Eyota teased as she followed behind.

Justin and Eyota had been friends for a year now. They had learned how to have a firm brother and sister relationship, but they were still learning as they went.

Eyota had grown up on the reservations, but when she was eighteen she had moved to the cities. Her Dakota features showed her raw beauty. Her long, thick black hair was braided, she had high cheek bones, deep brown skin (though that depended on how much time she spent in the sun), dark brown eyes that looked black at times, and she was tall and thin. Eyota had gotten saved when she was a teenager, and her relationship with God had changed everything. Her family had struggled with addiction, and Eyota was the first in her family to break free from that generational curse. Eyota had to be brave to travel on this new road. She learned how to rely on God for strength, and she had a strong moral compass.

Justin, on the other hand, was completely different in looks and temperament. Justin had curly blonde hair, green eyes, and he was shorter in height and muscular from going to the gym. He was also a bit more reserved and quieter compared to Eyota, who was energetic and outgoing.

Yet, they both got along great. They were able to connect deeper than most of their friends because of their similar family situations. Eyota's family had problems with alcoholism, whereas Justin's family struggled with drug addiction. Both had learned to break the curses that held their families hostage, and they often prayed together for the salvation and breakthrough for their families.

"Shouldn't I be telling you to slow down, Eyota? You are taller than me," Justin teased right back. They had such a wonderful and playful rapport with each other.

Eyota laughed, and finally they stood at the top of the mountain, admiring the view. As they did, Eyota wondered how she should venture into this new topic with Justin. Last week she had found out that he had started dating. Eyota was excited for him because she knew how long he had been waiting for the right girl. But they had never discussed how their brother and sister relationship would need to adjust to this relationship. 'Holy Spirit, give me the right words, please?' She prayed silently.

"By the way, I heard you started dating Janette from church. Congratulations!" Eyota figured she might as well dive bravely into the situation.

Justin looked over at her and smiled. "Thank you. I'm super excited she said yes. It's only been a week, but it feels like we've been dating for a lot longer."

Eyota smiled. "I'm glad your connection is so strong. I think it shows what God will do in and through you both."

"I think so too. We had been praying about it before we decided on it, and we even got godly counsel. I really think God is going to do some awesome things and I am excited to see where He leads us."

"I am excited for you as well. You know…I don't think we have ever talked about our brother and sister relationship and what changes we need to make when we're each in a dating relationship ourselves."

Justin looked over in surprise. "I don't understand. What needs to change?"

"A lot, actually. I just had this talk with Nick last week, so I know what direction we need to go in. You know how Nick and I met in high school and have been friends for ten years?"

Justin nodded.

"So Nick is about to ask a good friend of ours if he can pursue her, but he wanted to talk to me first because it would affect our relationship. What Nick said made a lot of sense. Can I share it with you?"

"Sure…I'm kind of surprised that you feel like something needs to change when I just started dating, but I would like to hear what Nick said about his own situation."

"I was surprised too, but as I listened to Nick it began to make sense. So let me just say it how he did. 'Eyota, I want to ask Amelia if I can pursue her, but I want to talk to you first because that will change our relationship. You and I have a very close brother and sister relationship, but it is important for us to honor the people we date and marry. If I am pursuing someone, but continue to have one-on-one connections with other women, I am not respecting her, and I'm leaving room for satan to slander my character. It could also make room for the one I love to misunderstand my character and my faithfulness to her. Now, I don't believe that I need to shun you or cut you off from my life, but when we text or call, etc., she will be in the room or in the group chat. When we hangout, she will be with us. So now we need to figure out how to be brother and sister with an in-law joined, does that make sense?' And it did make sense. I realized that Amelia would not feel loved by either of us if she knew that we were connecting one-on-one without her. She needs to have his heart first. Does that make sense?"

"I guess…I never really thought of it that way. I've just always maintained my friendships with girls when I was dating before. I guess I don't think it's necessary. The one I date should know my character and trust me."

"I don't think that's true, Justin. She shouldn't be forced to accept that kind of relationship. She should see that you are putting her first, that you are faithful, and that you have nothing to hide. When I get into a relationship, if my man won't do the same, then I won't be in a relationship with him. I want him devoted to me. I understand that you maybe don't feel the same as I do, but I want you to know that today will be the last time we hang out without your girlfriend or other friends present. I also won't be responding to one-on-one texts, but I will respond in group messages."

"I don't agree, but it sounds like you made your decision…so I guess I don't really get a say."

Suddenly I was Philip-Transported into a gym. I looked around, a bit surprised at the abrupt change from a mountain top to a gym.

Chapter 14

I looked around in surprise. To be honest, I was wondering if maybe the Holy Spirit had mistakenly sent me to a wrong location, but then I laughed at my own silliness because I know the Holy Spirit never makes mistakes.

"Holy Spirit, who am I supposed to watch now?"

"Do you see the couple on the treadmills?"

"Yes, they seem to be doing their own thing, but I can tell that they are together."

"Aubrey, I want you to observe."

"Okay, Holy Spirit."

I made my way closer to watch.

Parker and Sophia had been dating for two years now. They met their junior year of college and now that both had graduated, Sophia was hoping Parker would be interested in bringing their relationship closer to marriage.

Sophia had a very religious upbringing, being from the Bible Belt. She knew the Bible forwards and backwards, she knew which verses to use for correction, and she knew the importance of keeping up a godly appearance. Her parents wanted nothing to tarnish themselves in other's eyes. Sophia had a wild mane of hair, and, living in the south, had learned how to tame the frizz. Her chocolate brown eyes and porcelain skin were the perfect balance to her wild personality.

Sophia was outgoing and had grown up in such a religious, legalistic family that her relationship with God had been based more on laws than actual relationship. It wasn't until recently that she began to understand that God wanted a personal relationship with her as a Father and daughter.

Parker had also grown up in the Bible Belt, but his family was the complete opposite of hers, with the mentality that anything goes. Parker and Sophia had talked about it before, how it seemed his family believed they could do anything they wanted because all they had to do was repent and ask for forgiveness. Parker was tall and well-built, and with red hair, hazel eyes, and fair skin, he stood out next to Sophia. Parker also wore round glasses and had a nerdy look to him, though he also enjoyed the gym.

Both were running on the treadmill and every so often would glance over and smile at each other. There was a silent connection between them, where no words were needed. They just enjoyed their time together.

I kept watching, but nothing was out of the ordinary. I thought maybe I was missing something, but I didn't understand what it could be.

"Holy Spirit, am I missing something?"

"On the outside, it looks like everything is good between them. They look like a normal couple, fully in love and supporting one another without doubt or question."

"That isn't the case?"

"No, their issue is an inward problem. It goes so deep that most would not see it."

"How can I observe it then, Holy Spirit?"

"Aubrey, I'm opening your ears to hear what is taking place inside of them."

Immediately my ears were opened. All of a sudden, I could hear both Sophia and Parker's thoughts. The rush of information was overwhelming.

"Holy Spirit, it's too much! Can I hear one at a time?"

"Yes, let's listen to Sophia first."

I nodded and focused in on Sophia's heart:

"God, I know that You want a relationship with me, but I don't think I can be fully honest with Parker like You probably want me to be. I was so young and rebellious during my teenage years. I hated the legalism I was under, and I admit, I really wanted to act out against my parents. It was never my plan to get pregnant at seventeen, God. I honestly didn't plan on it, but You know that there was no way to tell my parents that. I can't even imagine what they would say even now if they knew. I know that abortion is wrong, but at that time, I….I didn't know what else to do. I know that You have forgiven me for taking my child's life, but I can't tell Parker about it. I'm just going to let this secret be between You and I, okay God? Just You need to know about it. I'm never going to tell another soul here on earth about it."

I gasped in surprise, but not because she had an abortion. I knew all along that the old church had been doing a horrible job helping women who had made a mistake, or even those who were a victim of sexual assault and gotten pregnant. Many times the church will become full of gossip and harshness, and cast judgments on the women, so that most of them would rather remain silent than open themselves up to the church. Yet, that is exactly what they need to do, so that the church can be there to help them and show them that there are other available options and that murder isn't necessary. My heart was broken for the child who would never be allowed to reach all that the Father had designed them for. A child who was supposed to leave a mark on the world, transforming it for the Kingdom of God. I felt great sorrow too for the fact that she was going to keep this information from Parker instead of being open and honest with him.

"Now it's time to hear Parker."

I nodded and listened.

"God, You know that I have had bipolar disorder since I was a teenager. I have worked hard to keep it hidden, and created habits that help me limit the severity. I know I still have days where it can get really bad, but I have been able to maintain a pretty balanced emotional life. God, I know I need to tell Sophia, but I'm going to wait until we are married. I don't want her to be scared or push away from me if she knows before. I think we need to have the commitment there first, and that will help her resolve to stay with me. I know You desire us to be open and honest and I will be, but I am going to wait till we get married."

"*What*? Holy Spirit, both of them are hiding such big, important matters. Their whole relationship is built on mistrust, and neither are truly loving or trusting the other person."

"You are right, Aubrey. Both of them are allowing fear and distrust of the Father and each other to keep them from walking in obedience. Both of them are so scared to show their true selves now that they have put on masks to hide who they really are. When they get married, they will be in for a rude awakening.

"I want to take you to the next observation. This couple has a similar situation in the fact that it is an inward heart issue. So keep your eyes open and observe very carefully to see the full picture."

"I will, I'll watch carefully and if I have questions, I will ask You again."

With that I was Philip-Transported to a restaurant. It was full of business executives and their spouses or significant others.

Chapter 15

Straightening my dress, I realized that this restaurant was completely different than the Chinese restaurant I had visited before. This one had an Italian flare to it. It was rich in culture as well as color. There were deep earthy tones on the furniture and walls, with the elegant use of white and gold accent pieces throughout. Murals of a Medici villa were painted on the longest wall, giving the space a larger feel.

The noise of the executives drew my attention. They were robust in their business talk and I noticed that there was an even amount of men and women. Most of the spouses or significant others sat listening to them talk, and some had grouped together talking about kids, sports, etc. I noticed one girlfriend sitting alone at a table. She stood out to me and I knew she was one of the people I was to observe. I made my way closer and sat at another table with a good view and within earshot. "This is the one, right, Holy Spirit?"

"Yes, Aubrey, good job listening."

"Alana, why are you sitting alone here at the table?"

Alana looked over and noticed her boyfriend's boss's wife, Tamara, making her way over.

"Good evening, Tamara." Alana tried to put on a smile that would hide the fact that she and her boyfriend, Ben, had just had a horrible argument before coming in. Although they had been dating for over a year now, it felt as if they knew each other even less than before.

Alana had tried over and over to keep the peace and to learn Ben's expressions, because she knew he hated being asked how he felt. In fact, she had gotten very good at reading his facial expressions and nonverbal cues, and she was beginning to understand how much of his lack of conversation skills with women was from what he had experienced growing up. His dad was very closed off and distant from his mother, and Alana could see that history was repeating itself.

"Good evening. How have you been lately?" Tamara smiled at Alana. The young woman reminded her of herself when she was young. Not so much in looks, but in temperament and character. Tamara had rich dark skin, black eyes, and black hair. Alana was a tanned, blonde-haired, blue-eyed beauty. Although she had amazing looks, Tamara could tell that didn't matter to Alana. She had actually observed that Alana never used her beauty to manipulate or get attention. Instead, she carried herself with elegance, confident in who she was, and used her skills of communication to build connections. Tamara had always thought Alana and Ben were a power couple. Ben worked in financing, and Alana was a reporter.

"I've been doing good. It's been really busy at work."

Tamara nodded. "Ben mentioned to my husband that you were in Israel reporting on the war."

"That is correct. It was a very eye-opening experience to see for myself that everything my own country has been saying about Israel and judging them for has been so wrong. I saw the aftermath, but I also saw what Israel was before the war. Ten years ago, I went to Israel for a tourist vacation with my family. I was amazed at how the Jewish people, the Muslims, and the Christians could all live in Jerusalem peacefully. I felt safe walking around with them. Of course, as in any country you have to be careful about where you go and when, because evil is around us in every country. But I absolutely loved seeing how they could all be there together, and I didn't feel shunned or uncomfortable. I actually felt uncomfortable because of other tourists who didn't respect the culture they were in. They were so loud, and their clothing made me blush in shame."

"I never thought about that. I'm sure it's hard coming back here after witnessing the devastation that took place against the Jews and then be treated like you're a liar back here at home.

Most Americans have a herd mentality and they follow without actually thinking or doing the research themselves. The terrorist attack against the innocent revealed the evil that resides in many Americans' hearts."

"It's true. There's a level of deception and depravity that runs deep in American hearts, and it is eye-opening. As a reporter I saw the horrible evidence of the wickedness of Hamas. And you know the sad part? I feel for the Palestinian people. They are suffering now from the actions of the leaders they put into office. So now you have people suffering on both sides, but Hamas cannot be in power. If Hamas is in power, no one in this world is safe, but when Israel is in power there can be peace, and the people will be provided for. But that would require the Palestinians to accept the government. The Bible makes it clear that Israel, the Jewish people, will remain because the whole book of Revelations will take place in Jerusalem and in Israel.

"The most ridiculous and bizarre thing I have witnessed since coming back to America is those who support Hamas. Many of them are gay/lesbian, transgender, pro-choice, woke, pro-socialism, and antisemitism. The truth is, if Hamas and other Islamic extremists took over, they, alongside Christians, would be the ones taken outside their homes, and experience the exact same things as Israel. Homosexuality, sex before marriage, and even the clothing many women wear all go against the Islamic law. So don't you think that if they were to ever take over America, people who have different beliefs would not be allowed to live or would be forced to come into alignment with their beliefs? Yet, so many in America would never believe that would happen. They have almost romanticized terrorists and those whose actions are the very incarnation of evil. They call that which is good, evil, and that which is evil, good.

"In the Quran, Sarah 2:191 says, 'Kill them wherever you come upon them and drive them out of the places from which they have driven you out. For persecution is far worse than killing. And do not fight them at the Sacred Mosque unless they attack you there. If they do so, then fight them—that is the reward of the disbelievers.'[4] Again in Sarah 9:5 says, 'But when the forbidden months are past, then fight and slay the Pagans wherever ye find them, an seize them, beleaguer them, and lie in wait for them in every stratagem (of war); but if they repent, and establish regular prayers and practice regular charity, then open the way for them: for Allah is Oft-forgiving, Most Merciful.'[5]

"Now, there are many Muslims who won't fall into the category of killing non-believers for their faith; however, within Islam, there is a great number of extremists who take these verses to heart, and their goal is to remove every person that doesn't believe the way they do."

Tamara quietly mulled that over. "I never thought about that before, but I see your point. Alana, are you sure that you want to write about these things? People will judge you, label you, and attack you."

Alana nodded sadly. "I know, but my relationship with God is very important to me. I have to speak the truth, even when the country doesn't want to hear it. Yes, I will be targeted and hated for what I say, but I must speak forth the truth, no matter the cost."

Tamara looked at Alana with pride. She knew the risk she was taking, and yet her bold pursuit of the truth was admirable.

Alana wished that Ben understood her more. In fact, they had been talking about this very same thing on the way here, and that was when they argued. Ben had no compassion for what Alana had just witnessed. He didn't care that her heart was raw or that when she closed her eyes at night, all she could see were images of the victims from the Hamas terror attack.

---

[4] "Quran" by Muhammad. Translated by Al-Baqarah. 2024.
https://quran.com/en/al-baqarah/191

[5] "Quran" by Muhammad. Translated by Yusuf Ali. 2024.
https://quran.com/9/5?translations=18,85,84,21,20,19,101,22,17,95

Alana glanced over at Ben. He was tall, with brown hair and green eyes, and he always looked professional. Alana felt broken inside. All she wanted was for Ben to see inside her heart, to have compassion. She longed for him to know her facial expressions, her non-verbal cues, and be sensitive to her. But after today's argument, she understood that he had no desire to do that. In fact, his words kept playing through her mind:

"Alana, give it a rest. I don't have time to talk about your experience. I will try to find time this coming week so we can sit down and talk, ok?"

"Sure."

"I know you just got back yesterday, but I really wish you were wiser with the timing of discussing these subjects. Right now, I really don't care what you saw there. I really don't want to know about it. So I hope you'll respect me and stop talking about this."

Alana had let the conversation end, but she also understood that it was an end to her relationship with him as well. He never wanted to hear her heart, or to let himself share his feelings with her. She wasn't looking for a business relationship, but a covenant relationship that would last her lifetime.

I silently observed Alana watching Ben. I noticed that Ben didn't look at her even once. He was so engrossed in talking about finances and work that he didn't have the time or patience for Alana. I noticed how annoyed he was that she was just sitting at the table by herself.

 I watched as Tamara made her way over to where her husband stood, talking with Ben.

"Ben, I loved talking with Alana just now. She really makes you think and view life from a completely different perspective. I especially appreciate her boldness and the way she stands for truth."

Ben looked at Alana with thinly veiled annoyance. 'I can't

believe she talked about that here,' he seethed silently. 'I'll have to correct her when I take her home.'

My heart broke in that moment. It was obvious that Alana was the only one in love. The relationship had become very one-sided.

Abruptly, I was Philip-Transported to a bar. Now, I had been confused when I was transported to the gym, but this blew my mind. Why was I at a bar?

Chapter 16

"Um...Holy Spirit, why are we in a bar?"

"That is a great question, isn't it? Sadly, in the old church it is normal for Christians to go to bars and drink and party."

This I understood. I had never thought that this lifestyle was pleasing to the Father. We are called to live in purity and be His ambassadors, and yet His people were going out to bars as if that was where the Father belonged. It would be different if they were going to share the gospel and salvation, avoiding the drinking and partying. But most Christians joined in the revelry, so being an ambassador went out the door.

"Aubrey, out of all the dating couples here together, which ones are believers?"

I looked around, ready to answer, and paused. The truth was, I had no idea.

"Aubrey, observe everyone here and see if you can find the Christian couples."

I nodded, feeling a tinge of nervousness, hoping one couple would let God's name slip so I could at least know if they were or weren't. It would all depend on how they used His name. Slowly, I began making my way through the crowd, listening carefully.

"Honey, I love what you are wearing today. You look sexy. Makes me want you," one man whispered seductively to his girlfriend. She blushed. "Thank you, I wore it just for you."

My eyes widened. I didn't think these people were believers. So I moved on, passing by a group of men.

"Look at my girlfriend over there. She definitely knows how to get a reaction from me," another man said, while the others laughed. "Yeah, your girlfriend definitely turns heads," one of them commented. "She is hot. Have you gotten her in bed yet?" They all laughed again.

I moved on. These men were not talking about things that would honor the Father. However, I was curious if the girlfriend they were talking about might be a Christian, so I made my way over to the girls.

"Your boyfriend sure knows how to drink. Does he ever get rough at home?" One girl asked the girlfriend. She laughed and replied, "Depends on what you mean by rough." All the girls giggled at the hidden innuendo. "He actually is very flirty when he's drunk," the girlfriend added. The other girls snickered.

I moved on, frustrated that I still hadn't found the Christian couples. I passed by some older couples, hoping maybe they were the ones.

"Sugar, how about coming home with me? You're too hot to be out on your own," one man said tantalizingly. The other couples started teasing them, "Yeah, you've dated for so long, at some point you gotta take the next step."

Again I moved on, but as I reached the end of the bar, I still didn't have an answer. None of the couples restrained their words. They were flirting about sex, and it honestly wouldn't have surprised me if each one was sexually active because of the way they treated each other and talked about sex and spending the night together.

"Holy Spirit, I honestly don't know which ones are Christians. I don't see Yeshua in any of them. Nothing coming out of their mouths is what Yeshua would say. The way they were seductively touching their girlfriend or boyfriend is not how Yeshua would treat them. I honestly don't have an answer for you. Instead, I am questioning every couple here and wondering then, if they call themselves believers, are they truly saved?"

I could feel the Holy Spirit's sadness and the heaviness of the

Father's heart as He watched those who said they loved Him blatantly break His heart.

"There are six couples here who claim to be Christians, and yet none of them are being the Father's ambassadors. Each one has laughed at sin or engaged in it themselves. They have lost what it means to be children of the Most High God. They have sacrificed their characters and morals for the desires of the flesh. They have grieved the Father's heart."

Instantly, I was Philip-Transported to a room with three solid walls and one wall made of glass. When I looked through the glass wall, I couldn't see anything. It was pitch black. There was nothing in the room, just white walls and gray cement flooring.

As I stood in this room alone with the Holy Spirit, I began to process the last four observations.

"Aubrey, before you observe the next couple, I want to talk with you about what you witnessed before."

I nodded in agreement. My heart felt heavy, and I looked forward to talking it out with Him.

"We noticed with Justin and Eyota that Eyota had an understanding of what faithfulness and love towards her brother's girlfriend looked like. She wanted to respect Justin's girlfriend and refused to give satan room to speak evil to the girlfriend and cause her to question both Justin's and Eyota's characters. Justin, on the other hand, was only thinking about himself, and refused to put himself in the girlfriend's situation. He thought trust should be given blindly no matter how the other individual acts, and that word is more important than action. Justin should have cared about his girlfriend's heart. He should have desired to protect her and love her the way that Yeshua loves His Bride. When a couple is dating, they need to change from single to a couple. Not just in word but action as well."

"I noticed that too. Justin was extremely selfish and only cared about himself. He didn't even care about his sister's feelings."

"Exactly, he was only concerned about himself. Next, we learned from Sophia and Parker. Both loved the Father, but neither of them were willing to walk in obedience. By hiding her sin, Sophia was actually refusing to walk in freedom and forgiveness, and was walking under condemnation, guilt, and shame instead. She was held hostage to her fear of revealing it to Parker. Parker, on the other hand was hiding his mental health. Instead of allowing Sophia to decide for herself if she would stay in the relationship, he was manipulating her by withholding the information until it was too late for her to choose. Neither of them were loving one another correctly. Neither of them were walking in trust. Their relationship was extremely flawed, and, because of their dishonesty, their relationship will not hold out once they are married because they will forever question if the other person is being honest, so when situations arise, they'll always question the other's character. Sophia and Parker will end up resenting each other, and neither of them will bring glory to the Father in their relationship. It will be broken. If both of them wait until they're married to be honest, truthful, and transparent, they will at least have the information out in the open. However, satan will still use it for the rest of their married life, and they will need to remain in the Father in order to overcome the door they opened to satan. The Father will still be glorified in their marriage, but they will face many battles that they would never have had to if they were just truthful when they started dating."

I nodded in agreement. Honesty is really the best policy. Yes, the other individual may choose to leave you, but I would rather have someone choose me knowing me fully, than choose me and always question if they would have if they'd known me.

"Aubrey, the next was Alana and Ben. I have witnessed so many girlfriends/boyfriends who refused to have compassion for the girlfriend/boyfriend. They refuse to go above and beyond and get to know the other person's heart, their facial expressions, and all their nonverbal cues. It's not only a problem with those who are dating and engaged, but it is also a problem in many marriages. At some point, they start doing the bare minimal and yet expect to spend their lives together."

"Ben missed the chance to hear about the fears that plagued Alana's sleep, the images she was struggling to move past. He missed the opportunity to support her heart and her calling to truth. Instead, he only thought about his own needs and wants, and he refused to accept the Father's truth. It's almost like he was siding with the world, and had forgotten that the Father warns that whoever curses and goes against Israel will be cursed and condemned. It's almost as if he was following the norm and ignoring the facts staring him in the face. I felt really bad for Alana, but I know there are so many other couples out there who are experiencing the same thing. They are in a one-sided relationship and giving their all, only to be ignored and left to do all the work."

"That is a good point, Aubrey. Too many individuals settle for a boyfriend/girlfriend or a husband/wife just to be in a relationship, but they will find themselves hurting and unequally yoked.

"Finally, there was the last observation of six 'Christian' couples in a bar, and you still don't know which ones they were."

"It's true, Holy Spirit. I have no idea which ones were the Christians. They all looked like the world and sounded like the world, and there was nothing to indicate which person loves Yeshua and has relationship with the Father. They were sexually flirty, handsy, and kept hinting at sexual activity. They were all drinking beyond their limits, and lost all restraint. There was nothing about You there, and the only way I knew You were in that room was because You were with me. Ephesians 5:18 (NIV) says, ' [18] Do not get drunk on wine, which leads to debauchery. Instead, be filled with the Spirit...'"

"Too many Christians follow the world's standards of dating instead of following the blueprints the Father gives for the dating and engagement season. Now that we have discussed each observation so far, it is time for the next one."

With that, a light shone on the outside of the glass wall. I could just make out a church entrance with the sanctuary in front of me.

Chapter 17

I was a bit surprised at the scene in front of me. I had assumed that there would be five wrong relationships and then five right ones. Maybe the Holy Spirit was changing things up. I walked up close to the glass wall and listened intently for what I was supposed to observe.

"Good morning, Jonas and Zoe."

Jonas and Zoe looked up at Pastor Frank and smiled. "Good morning, Pastor."

"I hope you guys are ready for a great church service. Go ahead and make your way in, we'll start soon."

"Sounds good."

I observed Jonas and Zoe make their way into the sanctuary and sit down. They looked like a loving couple and appeared to have a great relationship with the Father. I could see how excited they were to be at church. Jonas was Caucasian, with blonde hair and blue eyes, and was muscular. He was dressed casually in blue jeans and a t-shirt. Zoe had brown hair, green eyes, and olive skin. She was wearing a halter-top dress, but the length reached the floor.

Pastor Frank walked up to the pulpit and the service began. Halfway through the sermon, he said something that completely took my breath away. In fact, I had to double check that I was still even in a church.

"I have been doing a lot of praying about some hard topics that have been presented to me. After talking it over with the board, we have decided that some of our bylaws need to change. I really believe that God is a God of grace and that He accepts us as we are, so the laws of the Old Testament really don't apply anymore, because now we're in a season of grace. His love covers it all and no matter what we do, He makes it good. So the topics that we'll be bringing to the next meeting for the church to vote to change are: homosexuality, and that as a church we will support and allow for such marriages to take place in our church; transgenderism to be allowed, and couples living together before marriage."

"Um...Holy Spirit, I heard that wrong....didn't I?"

"*No*! Nope, you heard correctly. This pastor is standing before his congregation lying to them and claiming that sin is good. The Father does have grace and He does accept you as you are, however, if you are truly in relationship with the Father you will change and become more like Him. Because sin and the Father cannot be one."

The service was over, and Jonas and Zoe were heading out of the church. The image in front of the glass window changed again to a living room. Jonas and Zoe were sitting on the sofa. The living room had a modern, minimalistic feel to it, and the walls were white, with mid-gray flooring.

"So what do you think? Now that Pastor Frank has affirmed living together, are you comfortable moving in with me, Zoe?"

Zoe nodded her head. "Yes, once I heard Pastor Frank say it's okay, I decided I wanted to move in with you."

Jonas smiled. "That is awesome. Let's let our parents know. I'm sure they won't agree, but we can at least tell them our pastor blesses us."

Zoe nodded in agreement.

Jonas called his parents first. Zoe listened quietly, a little bit nervous.

"Mom, Dad, Zoe and I have decided to move in together. I know that you both don't agree with this, but I promise you that we won't have sex till we get married. We have been engaged for six months and in nine more we'll be getting married. I know you might not agree, but it makes sense for us. Right now we're both paying for our own rent, food, etc., and it's getting expensive. Not to mention gas prices going up, and with how much we have to travel to see each other, this seems like the best financial decision we can make. Also today, our pastor said he supports couples moving in together before marriage. So our church supports our decision. I know this will be hard for you, but I hope you will accept it too."

It was obvious to Zoe that Jonas' parents were not happy, but since they were adults they couldn't do much. Next it was Zoe's turn to call her parents. It went about the same as Jonas's call. After notifying their families, Jonas and Zoe sat back on the sofa and let out their breath.

"Well we did it, we told them."

Jonas laughed. "Yes, we did."

I began to wonder if they would really be able to keep their word and not have sex. It seemed like once they moved in, they would be walking in sin, and it was only a matter of time before satan took more than a step, and instead went a mile.

"Aubrey, I want us to go ahead a month and observe how they are now that they have been living together."

I nodded in agreement.

Jonas and Zoe were sitting at the dinner table, eating and laughing together. The modern theme of the living room carried into the dinning room as well. The dining room table was glass, with black metal twisted together to form a sphere base, while the dining room chairs were metallic with high backs and swooping back legs. The flooring here was gray and the walls white, and black and white modern artwork covered the walls.

"By the way, my parents asked if we were still abstaining from sex…I told them to stop worrying, we're still not having sex," Jonas said, laughing.

"My parents keep asking too. I wish they would just trust that we're able to keep ourselves under control and refrain from sex." Zoe rolled her eyes.

"Hey, let's watch a movie tonight."

"Sounds good to me."

Pretty soon they were sitting down, watching a romantic movie since Zoe got to pick this time. Thirty minutes in, Jonas lost interest in the movie, and instead wanted to kiss Zoe a bit. They had learned when they needed to stop in order not to cross boundaries. Jonas moved closer to Zoe's side, and, getting her attention, asked with his eyes if he could kiss her. Zoe smiled and lifted her head up to receive his kiss.

Jonas took Zoe's chin in his hand, and brought his face close to hers. Soon his lips gently touched Zoe's. Jonas was quickly dissatisfied with gentle and he began to deepen the kiss, sliding his tongue into Zoe's mouth. Zoe gasped in surprise, but she was thrilled by the deeper connection. Soon they were in an all out make-out session, and their hands were beginning to roam over each other's bodies, hovering over areas that they should not touch.

I watched silently as everything inside of me cried for them to stop in time. But soon I watched their hands touching places they shouldn't. Jonas stood up and pulled Zoe into his arms, lifting her up. And as they continued their passionate kissing, Jonas began to walk towards what I knew was the bedroom.

"NO! STOP!" I pounded my hands against the glass. Over and over, until my hands felt raw and bruised from trying to smash it. *"NO!* You guys need to stop. *STOP! STOP!* Don't do it. Do not cross this line. *STOP!"* My knees buckled and I crumbled to the ground, but I kept on shouting at them and banging on the glass. Yet all I could do was stare in horror when they didn't even acknowledge me. My attempts to gain their attention were all in vain. They made their way to the bedroom, and I watched as the door closed.

I was completely out of breath. My screams had left my voice raw and raspy. Tears were pouring down my face.

"Why, Holy Spirit, why didn't they hear me? Why didn't they stop?" I wailed.

Chapter 18

I felt the Father's arms surround me, and the calming voice of the
Holy Spirit began to speak.

"Aubrey, I know how badly you wanted to get their
attention. I know that you longed to keep them from
repeating your own mistakes."

"WHY? Why didn't they hear me, Holy Spirit?"

"They had already removed My conviction from
their life. They were already compromised and when
the sexual part of love blossomed, they were not
strong enough to stop. They had removed Me, and
their belief of right and wrong had already started to
shift long before this sin."

I couldn't stop the tears from falling. "Don't they
understand what they are doing? Don't they know they are
opening a door to satan that he will use for the rest of their
lives? Don't they understand the consequences of their
choices?"

I was brought back to my own sin. Before my ex-husband and
I had gotten married, we had been sexually active. It was used as
a form of control and I felt like I needed to keep giving sex so he
wouldn't leave me. There was also a high from having sex
outside of marriage, and the secrecy that went with it. However,
conviction, shame, and guilt rode close behind that high. When
we finally did get married, we eloped, and it was an area that
satan tried to use to keep me from the Father. I questioned my
ex-husband's love for me constantly, wondering if he would still
want to be with me if I hadn't given my virginity to him. I
questioned our relationship and his heart for me, and I realized
that because we had sex before marriage, it was no longer a
sacred thing. He ended up having a sexual affair right before our
two-year anniversary. I found out about it the day before my
anniversary. It was in that moment I understood that to him sex

was just sex, and there was no intimacy or meaning behind it. He didn't treasure intimacy with me, and he looked for pleasure in other ways.

I had opened the door to satan, not realizing that he was stealing the future the Father had for me. The effect on our marriage was long-lasting because it is a spiritual matter. And whether we want to admit to it or not, sin always has consequences. For eight years, my ex-husband would withhold sex for long periods of time as a form of abuse. He purposefully refused to meet my sexual needs and would find ways of meeting his own. As I mentioned before, it affected my relationship with the Father, because I knew I had made a mistake. I knew what I did was wrong. I knew that I had chosen sin and desire over Him. I had a lot of healing spiritually, perspectively, and physically that needed to take place; the Father took me through those times of healing during the three years after my divorce.

"Holy Spirit, they have no idea they are forsaking the Father's best by doing this. And although the Father can turn it for good, there will always be a consequence, and satan will always use that area as a weapon when he attacks. His assault will focus in on the sin, his attack will be targeted at the disobedience to the Father, and although they will receive healing, forgiveness, and freedom from it, they will still have to face the enemy's attack regarding it. They have no idea that they are giving up the best that the Father has for them."

I remembered how my relationship with the Father had changed because of my sin. I honestly had no idea how that sin would affect my life until I was divorced and saw my life for what it was.

"Aubrey, there are many countries where sex outside of marriage is considered criminal behavior. There are countries where although there's no law against it, the people of the country believe it's wrong. There are other countries where the people are mixed in their belief of it. The world has a lot to say about this topic, and even research done in 2002 by the National Survey of Family Growth shows that, 'Almost all Americans have sex before marrying.[6]'

"That means that regardless of if they are believers or non-believers, most Americans are having sex outside of marriage. For those who are not in a relationship with the Father, it makes sense that they would be living in sin. They have not come into redemption and forgiveness, and are unaware of their own sinful nature. Believers, on the other hand, have become deceived and allowed the flesh to rule instead of walking in their new man. Their spirit came alive when they came to Yeshua, but those who chose to sin, chose satan over the Father."

I thought about my own choices as I listened to the Holy Spirit. I had given up my virginity and had chosen flesh over the Father. I thought back to David's story and his struggle with porn and self-pleasure. I thought back to the years where my ex-husband would abuse me by withholding sex and the times where I self-pleasured to release desire after months of it being withheld. I thought about the guilt and shame it brought because I knew my ex-husband didn't want me or desire me, and didn't want to love me by meeting my needs like 1 Corinthians 7:5 said to. I thought about the anger, that I was being put in a position where my needs weren't met. I had to learn how to forgive my ex for making me feel the way I felt about myself, for the abuse, and I also had to forgive myself for choosing something that didn't honor the Father. I then had to battle to overcome areas of sin, and create habits to keep from falling into sin.

"Aubrey, so many believers have altered their

---

[6] "Trends in Premarital Sex in the United States, 1954–2003", by Lawrence B. Finer, PhDa. 2007. https://www.ncbi.nlm.nih.gov/pmc/articles/PMC1802108/

beliefs due to the culture and world, so they do not understand that it is the Father who tells them what is wrong and what is right. But even though they fall into deception and change their beliefs, it doesn't change what is right and wrong.

"The Father is the only one who determines what is right and wrong, and nothing man does will change that. Therefore, those who remain in sin will have to face the Father and deal with the consequences for it. Do you remember how in Song of Songs 2:7b (NIV) it is written, '7b Do not arouse or awaken love until it so desires,'?"

"Yes, I remember, Holy Spirit. In fact, it's written three times in Song of Songs (Song of Solomon)."

"You are right, it is written three times. Three is an important number."

I smiled because I knew how important three was in Biblical meaning.

"Aubrey, these verses are about more than just love, the feelings and emotions. It's more than just wanting a relationship. It's also about the physical part of love. It's combining sex with love and creating intimacy. You see, the Father created all of you to multiply the earth, yes, but He also created you to enjoy intimacy in sex. In 1 Corinthians 7:5 the focus wasn't to have sex to make babies, but to avoid falling into temptation and sin. The Father gave these warnings because He understands that once your physical body experiences sex, it will forever crave the wonderful feelings. The Father never meant that pleasure to be experienced before marriage with multiple people. He created that amazing experience that your body will always remember for one person, the one you will spend forever on earth with. That is why He doesn't want His children to arouse physical love (sex) or awaken it, because once it is awakened it will not go to sleep again. That desire, the memory of the feelings, and everything that goes with sex will be used by satan as temptation until you marry. Then after marriage it will be used as guilt that you didn't wait like the Father told you to. Satan is cunning, and he knows that if he can get your physical body, which remembers the feeling, into temptation, soon your flesh will override the spirit."

"That makes sense. This last year I learned that our bodies were made in such an intricate way that our physical bodies remember trauma and will respond to those same memories without our minds actually thinking about it. So my body basically turned on itself and went into survival mode, even though my spirit and my mind are the healthiest they've ever been. I had to start creating habits so when my physical body remembered things, it would have new habits to go to instead of the old. So it would make sense that our bodies would remember pleasure and the desire of sex. Within marriage, it's healthy and the way the Father created us, but outside of marriage it's lust and sin. Honestly, that was the biggest surprise I wasn't prepared for when I got divorced. I wasn't prepared for how my body remembered pleasure and sex. I had to work to create habits so I wouldn't fall into temptation. Sex in my marriage was about creating a baby. It wasn't about intimacy, it wasn't about meeting each other's needs, it was for the sole purpose of creating a baby. I remember clearly the last time I had sex with my ex, right before his last 'living as a single man' situation took place that led to our divorce, and in that last time I actually cried during it. I knew what was lacking and that the experience I was having wasn't out of love and intimacy, but out of the need to create life."

"Aubrey, the Father created intimacy in sex to be a very special and powerful experience when done right (within marriage) and with love. So we have learned that sex outside of marriage is sin. We have learned that self-pleasure is not of the Father either. One of the reasons I brought up the warning of not awakening love is because of what happens to men and women when they have sex. Many Christians have fallen into deception, and some have refused to acknowledge that there is a spiritual realm. For those who understand that there is a spiritual realm, this next revelation will be easy to understand. There is a connection made to each sex partner. There will be memories, pictures, smells, and emotions attached to these partners. All of these will bring that individual and experience back to mind. There is a soul-tie that connects you to that individual or individuals, and you will need to break off those ties through spiritual warfare. Isn't this proof of how important it is for sex to be with just one husband/wife for the rest of your life?

"This gives even more power to the warning 'don't awaken love.' The Father never intended for women or men to have so many soul-ties. He longed for His daughters and sons to have only one soul-tie. He doesn't want his children laying in their marriage beds and remembering past men/women they had sexual relationship with. It brings a whole new revelation about having only your husband be the one you think about and how he will have your back and protect you. Part of your healing process, Aubrey, was the Father took you through a time of spiritual warfare where you broke the soul-tie that bonded you to your ex-husband. That soul-tie needed to be cut off so you would not bring him into your next relationship.

"Aubrey, the truth is that many believers, both old and new, who have just come into relationship with Yeshua and with the Father have already had sex. Just as you mentioned that your body remembered, their bodies will remember too. For some, it has become a habit they have formed and fed that they are going to have to overcome. Others will have a sexual addiction. Some might be set free right away, while the Father will take others on a journey to freedom. It will require them to create new habits, new thought patterns, and learn self-control. And along the journey when they fall, it will require them to stand back up even when they feel guilty and ashamed. Instead, they will need to grace themselves, repent, and apply the right habits again until one day they will look at their life and see they have found freedom because it is no longer a temptation. They will need to cut off all soul-ties through spiritual warfare. It will be important to find Christian (Bible based) organizations, curriculums, counselors, etc., who will be able to walk them through the journey of freedom and healing. The point is that there is hope and freedom, and the Father will realign them back to His original design."

"I get it, Holy Spirit. Basically, if you have not had sex, don't, wait until you are married. If you have, then repent and sin no longer, by not having sex outside of marriage or doing self-pleasure."

"Simple, and yet the application is so very hard at times, Aubrey. But, it's also so very worth it."

"I agree. Holy Spirit, I am going to do it right this time. I am going to wait until I am married, and I am going to let my future husband know that he is worth waiting for."

I could sense the joy my words brought to the Father.

"Aubrey, it's time to continue our journey." And with that, I was Philip-Transported to a University.

Chapter 19

Going from a kneeling position to a standing position threw me for a loop. I looked around in surprise as I found myself in a University classroom. The classroom was emptying of students and only a few were still putting away their things.

"Holy Spirit, who should I watch?"

I felt the Holy Spirit nudging my spirit to a young woman sitting alone. She was so deep in thought she wasn't even aware of others around her. I made my way closer and sat down to observe her.

"Aubrey, I want you to hear her heart." And with that my ears were opened. This time it wasn't overwhelming, and I knew what to expect. I turned my head towards her and listened.

"I really hope that Do-Yun doesn't know about my feelings for him. God, I know that I just met him a couple of months ago, but as I have gotten to know him, my feelings toward him have changed. I see the man of God he is. I see how he cares for others around him, he acknowledges You in all he does, and he has great respect for the women here at school. He guards his tongue, and I have never heard anything dishonorable come out of his mouth. He actively makes You a part of his day, and he is always talking about You with others. He is so passionate about You, and I am really drawn to him, God. It's not just his looks, although I'm definitely drawn to his dark brown eyes, black hair, and fair, beige skin, and yes—it doesn't help that he works out and his body is in great shape, but I am not just attracted to that. Truth be told, God, although I appreciated his looks, I wasn't drawn to him until I knew his character. Who he is on the inside is what has pulled me in.

"But God, I don't want to lead this. I really want him to be the one to lead this. When I have prayed, You have told me to wait. I really hope that he hasn't recognized my feelings."

I sat back with admiration. Although it's not wrong to let a man know you like him, I loved how she asked God for direction and was being obedient to what He told her. I knew that wasn't easy.

"Aubrey, Do-Yun is a transfer student from South Korea. Adelyn has been seeking the Father about him for awhile. She has listened to everything I have told her to do."

I looked at Adelyn and admired her courage and her love for the Father. She had beautiful blue eyes, brown hair that curled in tight ringlets, and beige golden skin. Her eyelashes were long and curved naturally upward. Her eyebrows were full and lush. She had a dimple in her cheek that appeared when she was happy or mischievous.

"Aubrey, I want you to observe Do-Yun now."

I nodded in agreement, and was Philip-Transported into a dorm room. As I looked around, I straightened my dress. When my eyes landed on Do-Yun, I recognized him right away from Adelyn's description. He was with another male, and they seemed to be in a deep conversation.

"John, I've been praying about asking Adelyn if I can pursue her."

John nodded in approval. Both young men had noticed in the last couple of weeks that Adelyn had started to change how she responded to Do-Yun. Although she never told him directly that she liked him, it was obvious to both John and Do-Yun that she did.

"Do-Yun, what do you mean by 'pursue her'?"

Do-Yun smiled and gave thought to how he wanted to respond.

"I know that many guys, and girls for that matter, are okay with dating just to be dating. But I have never felt that way. I have been waiting for the one that God has for me. I told God that I wanted to pursue one girl, and that as she got to know me, then we would become boyfriend and girlfriend, but the end goal of that relationship would be marriage. So even though I know Adelyn likes me, I want to pursue her first to show how precious she is. Then after she knows my thoughts more, ask her to be my girlfriend, and then from there I would propose, and then marriage. I don't take a relationship lightly. I do not desire to date different 'options.' I have always longed for there to be just one. I have prayed, and the Holy Spirit has shown me that she is the one.

"I asked the Holy Spirit if I should pursue her now, because I know she just turned nineteen. Although I'm a post-graduate student, I'm twenty-four, which is five years older than her, but the Holy Spirit said the age doesn't matter and it's the right time."

John grinned widely. "So what are you going to do?"

Do-Yun laughed. "I'm going to go find Adelyn."

And with that I found myself Philip-Transported to a pathway that ran through the university campus. I immediately felt the change in temperature, and a cool breeze tugged at my baby hairs that had escaped my ponytail. I could see Adelyn walking, and coming towards her was Do-Yun.

"Adelyn, could I speak to you for a moment?"

Adelyn nodded nervously. *Please don't let it be about my feelings for you.* Her silent cry hit the heavens.

"The past couple of months, I have been watching you. Adelyn, you have so much of God's joy in you. You see the world through His eyes, and I am always amazed at the words God gives you for others and how they always line up to what is going on in their lives. I can see you have a deep relationship with God and I have enjoyed watching you interact with others around you. You are always encouraging, you speak truth boldly, and you don't shy away from hard topics but you also always do it with love.

"I have become very drawn to you. Adelyn, I would like to ask you if I can pursue you?"

Adelyn froze. She couldn't believe what she was hearing. Joy bubbled up inside and she felt as if she'd had the breath knocked out of her lungs. It took a couple of seconds for his question to fully reach her brain.

"Do-Yun, what do you mean by pursue?" She asked breathlessly.

"I'm glad you asked. I have no desire to be in a ton of relationships. I have never thought that was what God wanted for His children. I have always believed that if we are truly His, then we allow Him to be our matchmaker and bring us to the one He has for us. As we each let the Holy Spirit lead us, we are able to navigate the relationship He has for us. So what I am asking is, can I pursue you, and show you how precious you are to me, and let you see my heart for you? Then at the right time, I will ask to be boyfriend and girlfriend. But Adelyn, I want you to know that, following my pursuit of you, I want to take our relationship into to the next status of dating. The end goal, however, will always be a proposal that will honor you, and then a marriage that will last until we reach eternity."

Suddenly I found myself Philip-Transported to the ocean.

Chapter 20

"Aubrey, relax."

I realized my right hand was rubbing the scar on my left elbow. I purposefully relaxed my hands, and as my mind calmed I noticed my dress was blue now instead of black. The plumeria flowers were still white, though. Strands of hair blew in front of my face, carried on the ocean breeze. In that moment I noticed that my hair wasn't purple anymore. It was blue. The colors of the ocean rippled in the ombre locks of my hair.

I looked out at the ocean in front of me as the captivating waves unfurled. I could see thousands of beautiful shades of blue, royal blue, aqua blue, teal, turquoise, and Prussian blue blending and rising with the white foam of the waves. It was beautiful to behold. The sky was baby blue and the sun was a glorious gold. The fine sand was bleached white. I looked around me and noticed I was alone on this beach. The beach was surrounded by palm trees, hibiscus bushes, plumeria plants and frangipani flowers, creating a quiet sanctuary. One view was the beautiful plants, and the second view was the grand ocean.

After a time, I noticed that no one was coming for me to watch.

"Holy Spirit, who am I supposed to observe? There is no one here."

"Aubrey, we are going to observe you."

I stopped at that. I wasn't sure if I wanted to be observed.

"Aubrey, I was watching you during the last observation, and I already know what is going on, but I want you to talk it through with Me."

I nodded in understanding and felt the Father's love once again envelop me. I knew He loved me and He wasn't judging me for my thoughts, but was giving me the opportunity to move forward.

"You are right. The witnessing of their testimony made me feel both tense and joyful at the same time. Holy Spirit, when I first met my ex-husband, I thought he was one of a kind. He had the appearance of a man of God who was fully healed from his past. As we talked about before, I began to see his true attitude and character much later after dating, but by then we were already sexually active. I thought that all the words You gave me lined up so perfectly to him. The longing, Holy Spirit, the longing was so intense. The longing for a husband who would love me like Yeshua loves the church. A longing for a family to belong to, a longing for kids.

"As You know, I didn't handle the longing correctly. Instead of recognizing how Your words had shifted from him and were meant for another, I failed to see that You knew my ex-husband's heart and saw that he wasn't letting You move in his life. Your words were meant for someone else now, but I failed to recognize the shift and the changing of a season. I failed to be like the sons of Issachar (1 Chronicles 12:32), who understood the times and details of the Father. Because I didn't handle my longing correctly, I found myself thinking about things I shouldn't have. I started thinking more about sex and about kids, and I allowed the longing to propel me into a marriage I wasn't supposed to be in. I allowed the longing to take me away from the Father instead of to Him.

"You know what happened next. We eloped, and the following ten years of marriage were filled with his betrayals, the many times I was abandoned, the mental, spiritual, emotional, and sexual abuse I suffered. My longing took me into darkness, to a place of death where I was barely even functioning. My spirit was barely hanging on to the Father, and by the time He rescued me I was almost a completely different person. Those three years that followed my divorce were so beautiful as He healed me, restored me, and realigned me back to His original design.

"It was during this time that He placed a man on my heart. A man whose character and attitude drew me in. Not that his physical appearance isn't handsome, but I was first drawn to who he was inside and the outward only complimented that. He brought joy and laughter into my life. But, Holy Spirit, You know how scary that process was. To once again hear about the one the Father has for me. You took me through a time of learning to trust that I could indeed hear You and discern accurately who the words applied to.

"You told me to protect him and protect the word, not to let swine trample over it. So I pondered every word in my heart. I sought out accountability with my pastor, who is also my dad, and was open with a sister in Yeshua. In these years, I have kept Your words and Your promises. But I also protected my heart. I guarded my thoughts towards him, I kept my longing tucked deep down.

"Yet, now I am in a new season. The Father told me to write this book and He warned me that the longing would intensify. At first, I was scared that the longing would take over like before, but You showed me that I am not who I was then. You showed me that the Father has already taught and equipped me in how to handle the longing. So I bravely trudged through and found that I was pleasing the Father. The longing continues to intensify and yet it doesn't overwhelm me. I feel it so intensely and at times the tears flow wildly down my face, and it's even gotten to the point where I have to daily create a peaceful atmosphere around me, and yet it has drawn me to the Father.

"I have noticed that this longing has changed how I talk to

You each day. All of a sudden I will find myself in a deep discussion with You, and in ways it's like the times when I talk to You in prayer, but also it's very different. I realized that I have truly made You a part of my day, and because our relationship is that way, we communicate intimately. I don't have to position myself or ask You to talk, because I don't remove myself from You.

"You began to share about how it would be soon, soon the man and I would be connected, soon the door would open, soon. During this time I have realized how delighted the Father is with me. Then situations began to occur, and they looked the same as my experiences before. With my ex, his visa was running out, so I let the longing and pressure move me into marriage. Now I found out that this man the Father was speaking about needed to go away for a time. The pressure to do something, to make something happen was still there, but just like Adelyn, I recognized that the Father needed to do it, that He is the one who brings us together and receives all the glory from it. So I too remained inactive. I didn't pursue him or try to get him, but instead I have obeyed what You have given me to do instead. I am being obedient to You, and I look forward to the day his eyes are opened to me.

"Holy Spirit, I recognize that I truly am doing things differently. I am trusting the Father in a way I never did before. I am moving with You and I am confident in what I am supposed to do. I know how hard this is though. I know the weight it carries, and the emotions that come with it, but I trust You fully. I also recognize that if this individual does the same as my ex and won't let You be a part of his life, You will bring the one who will."

"Well done, Aubrey. You recognize how you have stepped into a new way of living in the spiritual realm. So although you are still doing the same activities and have the same responsibilities in the physical realm, it feels different because one day soon the physical realm will line up with what has already taken place in the spiritual realm. I want to ask now why were you getting tense?"

"I felt tense because even though I have peace and You have given me direction, and I trust You and keep my faith firmly in the Trinity, I still have deep feelings and emotions. But I recognize that just because I feel sad and disappointed that my time and the Father's time are different, the Father understands this. He doesn't judge me for the sadness and disappointment. Instead, You are all comforting me and letting me work through my feelings in a healthy way."

"Exactly! We see your heart, and we know your obedience. We are here to comfort you, and to help you continue in the active waiting, or as you and your sister-in-Christ, Krystle, call it, 'active courage.' I have told you that now you are running towards him, but it seems as if everything in the physical realm says differently. But I have seen how you trust Us. You hold on to what We say, you believe We will fulfill all that We have said. We have seen your obedience, your sacrifice, and your love for him and your love for Us. We are very pleased by you. You were made with feelings and emotions. You have learned how to feel and walk through them without allowing them to carry you into action or sin. I am proud of you."

In that moment, I felt the joy of the Father, Yeshua, and the Holy Spirit rush over me. I knew that although I still had to wait for the one, this time wouldn't be wasted. Instead, the Father was using it to adorn me so I would be presentable for my night with a king just as Esther was, and while the Father is adorning me, He is also preparing the one He has for me.

"Aubrey, well done refusing to let fear, anxiety, or nervousness keep you from what We have for you. I can see that you are now ready for the next witness."

With that, I was Philip-Transported to an art studio.

Chapter 21

I looked around at the art studio and was impressed. Colorful paintings of nature hung on the walls. On the left side of the studio was where artists could paint and explore different mediums, and on the right side of the studio was the pottery station and a display of pottery that had been delicately handcrafted. As I stood inside, I noticed a familiar couple making their way into the studio.

Do-Yun and Adelyn were teasing each other as they walked in.

"Adelyn, I hope you know that I am extremely uncomfortable and out of my element here."

Adelyn beamed up at him. "I know, honey. I really appreciate your willingness to try something I enjoy, though. It's a memory I won't ever forget."

Do-Yun gave Adelyn a loving smile. "Baby, I called ahead so they would have everything prepared for us. They told me we're to ask for Alissa."

I watched as they headed over to the pottery station. A smile spread across my face at the joy and love that filled the room. I could sense the Holy Spirit in such a strong way because He was also with Adelyn and Do-Yun. It was plain to see that they had made Him an active part of their daily lives.

"Honey, let's make each other a coffee mug!"

"Sure Baby, we can give it to each other at our wedding."

Adelyn laughed. "I can't believe we've been in a relationship for almost a year. You pursued me for three months, we became boyfriend and girlfriend, and then three months later you proposed, and now in three more months, we will be married. It feels as if this year has sped by, but other times it felt so slow."

Do-Yun laughed too. "I think we figured out this year that when the Holy Spirit is an active a part of our days, time is no longer the same. We are living in the Father's time, which changes everything."

I watched as they began to create their mugs and listened as they spoke words of encouragement to one another. Tears ran down my face at the beauty of this engaged couple who were clearly following the new blueprints the Father was giving me.

"Honey, I really am thankful that you take time to do things that I enjoy. I never feel like you're annoyed with me, but I can always see how you purposefully and diligently look for things we can do together that I enjoy too."

"That's because I see all the ways you create activities that I like, as well. You are also very aware of my needs, like my food allergies. Instead of getting sad when we can't go to some of your favorite restaurants, you lovingly look for new places that we can try and both eat at. Your heart for me fills me, and I want to fill you with the same amount of love. I also think we're finding that as we combine our interests and make room in our lives for each other, we end up enjoying new things. I know I have found some new hobbies for sure."

Adelyn nodded in agreement, a beaming smile on her face.

I watched as they completed their mugs and left them with the owner to finish the glazing processes. Soon I felt the Holy Spirit nudging me to follow them. I walked behind them as they left the art studio and headed to the park for a coffee date. Soon, coffee in hand, they sat down on one of the benches overlooking the pond that was in the middle of the park.

"Baby, I wanted to talk to you about something."

Adelyn nodded, giving Do-Yun permission.

"I am very thankful my parents traveled here to meet you before our wedding. I know it was important that both our families met. Something I noticed though, and think it's important for us to talk about now, is that some of the ways you talk to your parents isn't honoring. I know part of this is based on your culture, but because you will also be a part of my culture, this is an area that you will need to work on. Especially because I know your heart. I know you are not trying to be mean or come across as disrespectful to your parents or mine, but I don't want Koreans to misinterpret you when we go to South Korea. I want them to see how you are respectful and honoring to those who are older than you. I know you love your parents, but I personally felt hurt by your responses to your parents. Does that make sense?"

Adelyn nodded soberly. "I'm sorry. I wasn't aware I was coming across that way. I don't want your parents to think that way, or assume that I wouldn't be respectful to them. I know a lot of it is habit and the normal American way of living. It could be hard for me to recognize when I am coming across that way, because I am still learning about your culture. Please forgive me? Is there a way you can let me know without embarrassing me in front of everyone, but something just between you and I?"

Do-Yun looped an arm around her. "I forgive you, baby. Like I said, I know your heart and I know that this isn't who you are. Thank you for being willing to learn about my culture, and for being open to grow in areas that could become a struggle in South Korea. Let me think of a signal I could give you when I notice something."

Adelyn smiled contentedly, because she knew she was loved and seen, and that she didn't need to explain her heart because Do-Yun already understood. She also appreciated how she had learned to have better communication when feelings were hurt. Do-Yun showed the value of intimate communication in the way he was convicted and made things right, but also when she did something and he was hurt. It was something she had never experienced before, where they could communicate without anger or justifying themselves, but instead taking ownership of what they had done wrong and immediately making it right. It allowed for a stable, supportive relationship, and it gave each of them confidence in pursuing each other's heart.

I soaked in this beautiful moment. Do-Yun corrected in such a loving way, and Adelyn was so receptive and open to correction. I could sense the Father's adoration of their relationship, because they were applying their relationship with the Father towards one another as well. The Holy Spirit was active, and you could see that they were walking in spirit, not in flesh.

Chapter 22

Suddenly I found myself Philip-Transported to a mall. It was a busy time of day. I watched as crowds of people made their way past me. The shock of noise and visual stimulation was quite different from the quiet park I had just been at a second ago.

"Holy Spirit, who am I supposed to observe now?"

"Follow me, Aubrey."

With that, I followed the Holy Spirit as He led me through the mall until we reached a home goods store. I went inside and immediately my gaze was drawn to a man who looked like he was at the wrong store. He had the build of a football player, his hair was blond and spiked up short, and his blue eyes were fixed on a beautiful girl standing next to him.

Emily had long brown hair, tan skin, and brown eyes. Her build was long and of medium height. They both seemed to balance each other out. Jeremiah seemed bold and direct, and Emily was soft and gentle.

I drew close to witness the new blueprint.

"Emily, are you sure we need all new sheets, towels, and cookware?"

Emily frowned in slight annoyance. "Yes, Jeremiah, I am sure. Everything we have gotten to start our new life together are hand-me-downs. I want us to start a home that is new."

Jeremiah shook his head. "Darling, I think there are more important things that we could use for our new family instead of buying things God has already provided for. Granted it might not be the new style or color you want, but they meet what we need for now."

"But I want something new."

"I understand, but let's think this through. Okay?"

Emily still felt annoyed, but she knew that whether she wanted to or not, Jeremiah would share his wisdom. "Okay," she said with a sigh.

"Darling, right now I have one vehicle and your roommate gives you rides to get around. In five months we'll be getting married, and we will only have one car. Now, we can either spend some of the money we have been saving for a second vehicle on new towels, new sheets, and cookware. But if you decide that's the direction you want us to go in, then you need to know we won't be able to get a second vehicle right away. That means you'll need to find a way to get to work and back home everyday. We already agreed that since I work forty-five minutes outside of town, I would need a car no matter what.

"So I think it's important for you to figure out long term what is most important to you. I'm okay with either, but I also know both will require a sacrifice from you."

"Can I take a few minutes to think about it?" Emily asked, a bit convicted now. She had been so focused on what she wanted that she had forgotten what she needed.

Jeremiah smiled in encouragement. "I'll go check out the pricing for chairs and sofas we'll need in our new home when we're married."

Emily nodded and made her way to a quiet area of the store. She thought back to another time she had had a similar conversation with Jeremiah. He had been wanting a new TV for the house he was remodeling for them to live in. She had told him the same thing, "Do you need a new TV or furniture for our home?" Emily smiled at the memory. Even though a minute ago she was annoyed at being called out and corrected, she was thankful now that Jeremiah still chose to lovingly remind her of what was important. Emily had grown to appreciate that about Jeremiah. So many times she would be so focused on herself that she forgot there were two of them now, and they needed to do what was best for both of them.

Emily made her way to Jeremiah. "Honey, you're right. A car is definitely a need. I need to be wiser in how we spend the money we are saving."

Jeremiah smiled proudly at her. "I know how hard that is for you. Why don't you pick out a couple of your favorite sheets, towels, and cookware and add it to the wedding registry? Maybe one of our family members or friends would want to bless you with it."

Emily looked up in surprise. "I didn't even think about that. You are right, I could add it to the registry and let God work out my wants and if He wants to bless me with them. And even if He doesn't, I know I am still blessed and loved."

Jeremiah smiled wider. "I know it was hard to humble yourself and be willing to hear what I had to say, but I am proud of you for letting me share in the outcome of your choices."

"Thank you for being willing to support me in either situation, but I agree with you, sharing one car would definitely be stressful, and with wanting to start a family, it would be even harder with one car when you work out of town."

"You're right. We'd have to wait to have kids, and I know we both want kids pretty soon after we get married. I believe the Father will honor our choice to be wise with our finances. And I know that He gives amazing gifts.

"Darling, do you remember last week when I was picking out flooring for our new home, and I wanted wood floors in the bathroom?"

Emily laughed. "Yep, I remember."

"The Holy Spirit really convicted me during that conversation because I was really set with wood, and when you contradicted and gave all the reasons that laminate or tile would be better, I didn't respond well. The Holy Spirit reminded me that it was important for us to hold each other accountable, to let each other know the consequences of our choices and how it will affect our family, and that our communication should be truth in love.

"He also showed me there will be times where decisions are made that neither of us might agree on, but we need to keep building each other up. It's important that we encourage each other to make decisions that will bless our family. I want to be a husband that can receive wisdom, counsel, and correction from my wife. I don't want you to ever feel you don't have voice or that God hasn't given you wisdom and discernment, and I definitely don't want you to ever feel like I don't think you can hear from Him.

"So I really want to be a wise husband. I have also seen that you are willing to take my advice, and, like we talked about before, that you will submit to my decisions according to God's Word. I want you to know that I am trying my very best to make decisions for us, taking you into account, but mainly the Holy Spirit. Because I know that He will help both of us on this new journey."

I watched Emily and Jeremiah make their way through the store, and listened as Jeremiah teased her to be wise with the money.

Suddenly I found myself Philip-Transported to the backseat of a car.

Chapter 23

I looked around, quite surprised by my new surroundings. I curiously peeked over the front seats. It was a no-brainer that the two I would be observing were smack-dab in front of me.

I chuckled to myself. "Nice one, Holy Spirit."

Then I observed the two sitting in the front seats.

Anastasia was beautiful. She had blue eyes, wavy ash brown hair, olive skin, and was tall and slender. She was a professional dancer just like her mama, and had been putting in long hours at the dance company. They had just finished putting on a ballet performance telling the story of the nativity all the way to the Easter story of Yeshua. Now that the shows were done with, she was finally able to go on a date with her boyfriend, Ethan.

Anastasia looked over at him and smiled. They had been dating for a year now, and lately Ethan had been talking about marriage. She knew that any day now, he would be proposing.

Ethan was tall and muscular, and complimented Anastasia with his black hair, brown eyes, and tan skin. He was half a foot taller than Anastasia, but they fit together perfectly.

"So, Anastasia, are you excited to go to the new French dessert shop that recently opened?"

"I am so *excited*! It's been forever since I went to France with my parents, and I have been craving their macarons and profiteroles. I can't believe there's also a cute little bookstore connected to it. My friend was telling me that they have books from other countries and carry some classics as well."

Ethan grinned. Anastasia was glowing with excitement. He knew how long she had been waiting for today. She had planned this date months ago, and every week she would talk about it. Ethan knew how hard she had been working at the dance company and he was thankful that they could finally spend some quality time together.

Ethan parked the car, and they both made their way to the dessert shop. As they got close Anastasia noticed the lights were off. "Why does it look like it's closed?"

Ethan got to the door and read the sign silently with dread. 'Store Closed for family emergency! Will open again in a week.'

Ethan looked at Anastasia as she read it. Her eyes filled with sadness and disappointment. She didn't need to say anything for Ethan to know she was extremely disappointed. He immediately began figuring out how he could cheer her up and what they could do instead. Quietly, he sent a text to his aunt while Anastasia was looking through the windows. She wanted to at least get a glimpse of the inside.

'Hey Aunt Sherie, I was wondering if it would be okay if I took you up on the offer to ride your horses today?'

She replied promptly. 'Sure, Ethan. Come on over.'

Ethan sent a text to his mom letting her know of the change of plans. 'Mom, do you think you could pack a picnic lunch and bring it to Aunt Sherie's house in an hour? I'm going to take Anastasia riding and then I thought we could have a picnic by the lake.'

'Of course. I will quick get one ready and send it over. Have fun.'

Ethan took Anastasia's hand and led her back to the car. "I know you're disappointed. You've been looking forward to coming here for months. With every practice and show you performed, you were looking forward to this date as a reward."

Anastasia nodded sadly.

"I have an idea that we could do instead. Do you trust me?"

Anastasia studied Ethan and smiled. "Of course. Do I get to

know now?"

Ethan laughed. "Nope, you get to wait and see."

They got back in the car and Ethan followed the roads to his aunt and uncle's stables. Anastasia had not been able to visit there yet, so it would be a new experience for her. However, he knew she loved to ride. The last time she went riding was when her parents took her to England.

As they pulled up to the stables Ethan turned to watch Anastasia's reaction. Her eyes lit up when she saw the horses. "Do we get to go riding?" she screamed in excitement.

Ethan laughed at her joy and nodded.

Anastasia rushed out of the car, jumping up and down as if she might explode.

"This is my aunt and uncle's stable I told you about. Come on, let's go riding."

I watched as they both walked towards a midnight black American quarter horse, already saddled and bridled. Ethan helped her climb up. "Ethan, will you ride with me?" She asked eagerly,

With a smile, Ethan nodded and mounted up behind her. This was the first time riding double for him, but he enjoyed the close connection to her without it being sexual. They could just be close and enjoy the ride, and, having not had much quality time in the last couple of months, this was exactly what they both needed.

I watched from afar as they rode along the path leading to the lake. Thick evergreens and magnolias, maples, and oak trees surrounded the ranch. The lake was a fairly large one, and allowed for the perfect place to see the sunset in the midst of the forest. Ethan was doing everything in his ability to create an enjoyable memory for Anastasia. I followed along the path after them, enjoying the view and the closeness of the Holy Spirit.

"Holy Spirit, this is a beautiful view."

"Yes, it is. It's a reminder for you, don't miss opportunities to love one another."

I watched as they dismounted and Ethan led her to the lake where his mother had secretly laid out the picnic. I stayed at a distance as they laughed, talked, and ate. You could see that both were comfortable, relaxed, and enjoying each other's company. They obviously were treasuring this opportunity to be with one another.

Silently I observed as the sun began to set, the sky turned red and purple, and the atmosphere around Ethan and Anastasia became romantic and private. I watched as he got on his knee and proposed, and Anastasia jumped up and down screaming yes. I smiled at their joy and could feel the Father's joy too as we watched this scene.

"Aubrey, you are witnessing another beautiful story that the Father wrote. Each one allowed Me to lead them, and now you get to witness the fruit of their obedience."

I beamed as I witnessed the prayers of their parents and their own prayers be answered by our loving Father.

With a smile on my face, I was Philip-Transported back to the garden of my heart.

Chapter 24

As I stood in the garden of my heart, I noticed that a couple layers of wall had been removed. I still couldn't see over the wall, but it was being taken apart piece by piece.

"Holy Spirit, is it time to talk about the blueprints from the Father?"

"Yes, Aubrey. It is time for us to talk about what you witnessed and what the Father longs for His children."

"In my witnessing of the new I was reminded of the importance of negative observations. Can I share a few things that really stood out about those before going into the *witnessing* of the blueprints?"

"Of course, go ahead."

"I began to see that the Father's children have become very self-focused in a way that He never intended. The Father desires His children to focus on the other person's needs, because He knows that if every child is doing that, then all their needs will be met. For example, Justin didn't care about his new girlfriend, but if he would have put her needs first, and she did the same for him, they would find themselves fulfilled. I am starting to understand that, whether in a brother-sister relationship, dating, or engaged, we can be filled up in the right way if we each do our part. But when I look at the Father's children, so many refuse to do that. They go either to the extreme where they only put themselves first, or the other extreme where they are so focused on others that their own health and hearts are suffering. The Father truly wants us to be poured out, but also filled at the same time. When we are continually drained from, eventually what we pour out loses its significance, especially when we are not taking the time with the Father that we are supposed to. Ultimately, we need to be in deep relationship with the Father. We need to have You with us every day, actively being a part of our lives. If we separate You from our daily activities then we will find that what we are pouring out is more of us and less of the Father.

"I also recognize how many of the Father's children have been taught to hide truth about themselves. They are worried the old church will ignore, shun, and judge them. On top of that, many old churches are not equipped to help them overcome sin, temptation, and trauma, and so they are left alone trying to fend for themselves. They then take this mindset into their relationships, when the Father has actually called us to be open and honest about ourselves. He wants us to be vulnerable with the one He has brought to us, the one we are to spend our lives with in marriage. But, because of the way the old church has handled such things, they are kept hidden.

"You also have the extreme where the old church says not to share those things because they are the past and you should not speak forth that which is contrary to what God says. Yet our testimony is where we were and what the Father has brought us out of. He is glorified, and so when we choose wisely who to share our pasts with, we actually bring honor to God and reveal the freedom we have truly been given. Being open and honest with both the good and bad in dating and engaged relationships is important. It's not a want or a need, but it's a command that we are to be a Bride who is honest and of integrity. If we do not apply it right away when dating and engaged, then chances are, it will not be applied in marriage.

"Our integrity and character are very important to the Father. He wants us to stand for truth, for justice, for the innocent, and for the things that He says are right. He wants us to condemn that which is evil, sinful, and wrong, but many of His children fail to do so. They are swayed by culture, wanting to fit in, and they forget they were made to stand out. Our integrity and character should show forth in our relationships. We should be showing the world what they are missing out on, not joining them in their incomplete, unfulfilling relationships. The Father's children really have it backwards. We are meant to lead the way in dating and engagements. We are to show that when the Father, Yeshua, and You are active in our relationships, everything changes. The world should be craving what we carry and should be wishing for what we have, not the other way around. It's time the Father's children start showing the world what true dating and engagements should look like.

"The Father is longing for His children to become pure again. He has said that self-pleasure, sexual immorality, and lust are sins. He is calling His children to come out of sin and into true relationship with Him and the one He has given them for their future. The truth is, we no longer have time to live with one foot in the world and one foot in truth. It's time His children make a true decision, because no decision is still a choice of flesh over the Father."

"Aubrey, you are right. No decision is a choice of disobedience in and of itself. Time has changed. The Father gives extra time when needed, but there isn't extra time for disobedience. His children do not have the time to try out different men/women to date for marriage. There isn't the time to try out living together to see if marriage is a good fit. His children no longer have time for this. That is why they should be allowing Me to be a part of their everyday lives. Because as they are obedient in fulfilling the plans the Father has for them, I can then perfectly position their future spouse in their lives, because both are following the leading of the Father spoken through Me.

"Perspective is key for this to work properly. Aubrey, if they are looking at brothers/sisters in Yeshua as brothers/sisters and not potential spouses, they will be able to have healthy relationships with them because they will be seeing them through the eyes of the Father. When they see them as a potential spouse instead of trusting the Father, they take the relationship into an area of unhealthy, unmet expectations.

"Now this does not mean they won't find them unattractive, but instead they will admire them and let Me lead them in it, for if they are fully submitted to Me, then I will help them walk through those times of admiration and attractions. I will help them keep the right perspective toward each other. They will need to remain in submission to me. It is very important that the Father's children begin to hear My voice and nudging like never before. For things will happen rapidly, suddenly explode, and so they need to be ready for these relationships to happen, but not solely focused on it. Instead, when His children are focused on His kingdom and bringing it to the world, it positions them for relationship. But when they are focused on relationship instead of His kingdom, they will miss steps they were meant to take, delaying and maybe even hindering the future relationship all together.

"The Father's children have forgotten the reason for being here on earth. They are created for intimate relationship with the Father, time spent in His presence. Remember the Father physically walked with Adam and Eve in the garden. He is a one-on-one Father, not some God up in the sky full of judgment and wrath that you have to strive to please in order to get a reward. No, while all were still in sin, He sent His Son to die, to rise and defeat satan, and to come back for a pure Bride. So He calls His children to live lives of purity and integrity, bringing Him full honor and glory, because living that way is the child's way of showing their deep love for the Father.

"When they walk in gentleness and kindness, letting the fruits of the spirit shine forth, they reveal Yeshua to that individual and to the world. Galatians 5:22-25 (NIV) says, '[22] But the fruit of the Spirit is love, joy, peace, forbearance, kindness, goodness, faithfulness, [23] gentleness and self-control. Against such things there is no law. [24] Those who belong to Christ Jesus have crucified the flesh with its passions and desires. [25] Since we live by the Spirit, let us keep in step with the Spirit.' It is so important for His children to live this way with one another, especially in relationships, to show the world the right way of being in relationship. This will show the world how to love someone, unveiling the truth of how to have a fulfilling relationship, where all needs are met.

"Everything you witnessed showed the importance of having a teachable heart like Proverbs 9:9 (NIV) says: '[9] Instruct the wise and they will be wiser still; teach the righteous and they will add to their learning.' You witnessed communication that showed teachable, humble hearts, those that understand the importance of putting the other person first instead of themselves. They communicated in love and gentleness, and yet still spoke the truth. You witnessed couples going out of their way to connect and create memories. When a couple gives to one another instead of one having to constantly bend, the world will see the Father glorified, because they will see a couple truly walking in the Father.

"You witnessed each couple meeting each other's needs, and being fulfilled, and it brought you joy as you witnessed it."

"You are right, Holy Spirit. It was beautiful to witness the gentleness and love that was shown. It made me ask, 'is this really possible, can I really have this?' I realized that the answer is, 'yes, I can,' because the one the Father has for me will also be listening to You. I like how Proverbs 19:20 (NIV) says, '[20] Listen to advice and accept discipline, and at the end you will be counted among the wise.' I want to be wise, Holy Spirit. I want the world to see Yeshua in me.

"I also loved seeing how each couple had a tight rein on their anger and annoyance. They displayed great self-discipline. It showed me again the importance of Proverbs 22:24-25 (NIV) which says, '[24] Do not make friends with a hot-tempered person, do not associate with one easily angered, [25] or you may learn their ways and get yourself ensnared...'

"As I think about it, I am beginning to understand the importance of the words You gave to John. 1 John 3:14-16 (NIV) says, '[14] We know that we have passed from death to life, because we love each other. Anyone who does not love remains in death. [15] Anyone who hates a brother or sister is a murderer, and you know that no murderer has eternal life residing in him. [16] This is how we know what love is: Jesus Christ laid down his life for us. And we ought to lay down our lives for our brothers and sisters.' When we are focused on loving others the way the Father wants us to, we find our own needs met as well. It's so beautiful to think about how the Father designed relationships. It also shows how the old church has failed, and it's time for new blueprints to be activated and for the Bride to rise up.

"Also, as I was listening to You, Holy Spirit, I began to understand something important. I was thinking about how quickly Adelyn and Do-Yun's relationship happened. It really was a 'suddenly,' but yet it was all aligned in time by You, because it was the Father's heart. I began to think about how it could work out for a suddenly to happen without the need for years to build a relationship.

"Even my own parents had a short time of dating and a quick engagement. Within a year they met, dated, were married, and then went to the mission field. I realized it's possible because as I speak in tongues to You (as discussed in Beyond Held Hostage) my own spirit and You, Holy Spirit, are having deep conversations. You are revealing things about my spouse to me. You are revealing his heart and his character to me. That means my spirit already knows my spouse, and so when we meet in the physical realm there can be a deep knowing of each other, because it was done first in the spiritual realm. Therefore I am known to him, and he is known to me. It shows the importance of speaking with You and talking in tongues even more.

"Romans 8:9 (NIV) says, '9 You, however, are not in the realm of the flesh but are in the realm of the Spirit, if indeed the Spirit of God lives in you. And if anyone does not have the Spirit of Christ, they do not belong to Christ.' I have You, Holy Spirit. So because I have You, I should also be listening to You and allowing You to lead me instead of ignoring Your existence. I also don't want to date many men to find the one. Instead, I choose to let the Father be my matchmaker, and I will follow You, Holy Spirit, as the

Father instructs You."

"Because of your decision right now, Aubrey, you will have a suddenly. We are proud of your decision and how you make Us the focus of your daily life. The Father is very pleased with you."

Part 3

Married/family Relationships

Chapter 25

"Holy Spirit, I am beginning to understand something very important about the observations. There is a difference between them and the witnessing You mentioned for the last five examples of both brother and sister relationships, and dating and engagement relationships."

"I love that you caught on to that. I knew you would."

I smiled at how well the Holy Spirit knew me. "I realized that the observations were focused on the wrong way of having relationships, while the witnessing had to do with the five brother/sister relationships and five of dating and engaged that showed the right way to have a relationship. I came to a deep understanding of the differences between them.

"For the observations, first off, the individuals did not have a committed covenant relationship with the Father. Second, they were not allowing You to be with them through the day. Which meant that none of them knew the Father's voice or Your leading."

"Exactly, Aubrey. None of them were living out their relationship with the Father. None of them were able to discern the Father's voice, My voice, nor what was right. Instead, they listened to the demons and followed the ways and responses of the flesh. For example, the pastor who spoke for satan instead of the Father. The couple used the demon's words to validate their decision, which clearly went against what the Father said was right. So when individuals aren't living out their relationship with the Father, and then get into a relationship thinking it will be a godly one, they will fall flat on their face because the

Father isn't a part of it.

"Aubrey, you are now ready to observe the marriage phase. As before, we will observe the wrong way, and then the Father will have you witness the new marriage and family blueprints."

"I'm ready, Holy Spirit."

With that, I was Philip-Transported into a dining room. The walls were painted off-white, with black and white paintings and portraits of flowers surrounding the dining room. A doorway to the east led to the kitchen, and the doorway on the south led to a living room. The north and west walls had large picture windows looking out at the backyard. The flooring was stained dark grey, which complimented the walnut furniture. A husband and wife were sitting down at the walnut rectangular table in what looked to be a heated discussion. I silently began to observe.

"Oliver, how could you even joke about that? I seriously can't believe you!" Chloe shouted, tears streaming down her face.

Oliver smirked at his wife, who was, once again, making a big deal out of a joke.

"Seriously, Chloe, can you just relax? It's just a joke, why do you have to be so sensitive?"

Chloe and Oliver had been married for a year and a half. At first Chloe liked the fact that Oliver had a sense of humor and enjoyed teasing and making her laugh. But it seemed like over the last six months, his teasing, his jokes, and his sarcasm were being used as a weapon in jest instead of done to make her smile.

Chloe was a five-foot tall, lovable, and outgoing girl. Although she was in her mid-twenties, youth glowed in her face. Her brown eyes, shoulder-length straight brown hair, and fair skin complimented her joyful positive attitude.

Oliver was a few years older than Chloe, yet in height he was only a couple inches taller. His black hair was buzzed short, and his tan skin and black eyes stood out next to Chloe's fair skin. Oliver was just as outgoing and loved to tease and be sarcastic with people. They usually brought out the best of each other, but lately it seemed as if they brought out the worst.

Chloe shook her head in disappointment. "I can't believe that you thought joking about having an affair was funny. Did you honestly think I would appreciate walking in to see you and Jane acting like you were having an affair? And secretly recording it to show friends? There is nothing funny about joking about an affair!"

"Chloe, they do it all the time in TikTok videos. Seriously, you need to relax."

"No, I don't. From now on I don't want you teasing about having an affair. It makes me feel sick to my stomach, and honestly, it makes me question your character."

Oliver was starting to get mad. 'I can't believe how uptight she is,' he seethed silently. Aloud, he snapped, "That just means you don't trust me or know me. If that's the case, where a simple joke changes your view of me, then we should just get a divorce."

Chloe froze and stared at Oliver in shock. Tears fell down her face. Her heart felt like it was shattering and her throat tightened as if she was being strangled.

Oliver winced the second the words left his mouth. He hadn't meant to say that, but his anger had gotten the best of him.

"You know what, Oliver?" Chloe's voice was trembling. "I am sick and tired of your jokes and your pranks that you pull with the intent to hurt me. You know exactly what I mean, because they're always about affairs, or leaving me, or divorce. You're even bringing up divorce right now in this argument. I can't do this anymore. I refuse to be hurt, manipulated, and abused in this way. I'm telling you now, if you ever pull another joke or prank, or bring up divorce out of anger again, we will need to separate and possibly even go to counseling before I would get back together with you. I refuse to be treated this way."

Oliver grew even more angry at Chloe's words. He shoved away from the table, went to the front door, and slammed it shut behind him. Chloe put her head down and cried.

As I watched, I felt the tugging on my own heart begin. How often I had heard the same teasing about affairs. How often the threat of divorce was thrown in my face during many arguments. I knew it was my ex's way of muting my words so that in the future I wouldn't argue and put up a fight against the abuse.

I watched as Chloe picked up her phone. "Mom," she said tearfully. "I don't know if I can do this anymore."

"What happened?" Her mom immediately asked, tone sharp with concern.

"Jane and Oliver played a prank on me. She had a tube-top on and was under the covers and it looked like she wasn't wearing any clothes. All that was showing were her arms and shoulders, and Oliver had his shirt off. They were recording it to put on his TikTok channel. It was a joke, but I honestly thought it was real. The fear, betrayal, and terror that filled my heart—I can't put into words how it made me feel. Now I don't feel like I can trust either of them. My husband who is supposed to be faithful, and my best friend, who would be willing to play such a prank on me! Am I reading into this, or am I right to feel this way, Mom?"

"No, you are right to feel this way. They crossed a line, dear. Do you want your dad and I to come over and sit with you for a bit?"

"Yes, please!"

Tears poured from my eyes. Her parents were so caring and supportive. It reminded me of my own parents and how they would protect me, even if it offended my ex. They knew they were called to be godly parents and it didn't stop just because their baby girl was married.

Suddenly, I was Philip-Transported to another house.

Chapter 26

I found myself in a kitchen. The kitchen was U-shaped, with dark gray bottom cabinets, and light gray top cabinets. The backsplash was white rectangular ceramic, and the countertops were black granite. The flooring was a rustic walnut laminate. Standing at the oven cooking was a man. I silently began to observe as his phone rang.

Nick answered quickly, putting the phone on speaker so he could keep cooking.

"Hello, sweetheart? When are you coming home? I am getting dinner ready."

"Actually, Lucy and Madelyn asked if I could go out with them tonight. So I'm just calling to let you know I won't be home until later."

Nick paused in his cooking, a pained look glinting in his eyes. "Oh, okay. Well thanks for letting me know. When do you plan on coming home?"

Over the phone, Blakely sounded annoyed. "I'm not sure. I will let you know later."

"Okay. See you later."

Nick finished cooking and silently sat down at the table. He began to wonder how long their marriage would last. After being married for five years, he thought they would last forever, but this last year Blakely had been going out with friends more and frequenting bars and clubs. It seemed she was no longer interested in being a wife. They had gotten married right out of high school, and now that they both had graduated from college, Nick had thought that they could begin to focus on having kids and a family.

Nick had been born into an interracial family, with a Kenyan mother and a Caucasian father. He had two brothers and they each took after their parents in different ways. His older brothers were darker like their mom, but Nick was a lighter shade of black. He still had black curly hair and black eyes, but his skin was more fair than his brothers', but, when he worked outside in the sun, his skin would darken more. Nick had grown up in a loving family, and the men always put their wives first. It was only natural for Nick to do the same, but it seemed that this year, Blakely pushed away from it.

Swiftly, I was transported to a local bar. It was a hopping, noisy joint. I saw a group of three women sitting together and figured that one of them was Blakely, but it was hard to know which one was married just by looking at them.

"I'm just so mad at Nick. Why can't he just let me live and have fun?" Blakely muttered to Lucy and Madelyn.

Blakely was wearing a tight dress that clung to her figure. Her long hair was put up in a clip, her make-up was dramatic, and her green eyes and fair skin contrasted the black minidress.

"I don't know, but it sure puts a damper on our fun evening," Lucy said. Madelyn nodded in agreement.

Blakely sighed. "I thought that being married would be fun, but I honestly didn't expect all the responsibility that comes with being a wife. Although Nick does help with chores, I just find the whole thing annoying. I know when I first told you I was getting married, you both suggested I wait till I was older, and I wish I would have listened. I feel like I gave up youth too quickly. I just want to hang out with you guys and have fun."

"Well, have you given anymore thought to what we said last time, about getting a divorce? I mean if you aren't happy and married life isn't for you, then why not?" Madelyn asked.

"I've thought about it. The idea grows more tempting by the minute. I keep imagining and daydreaming about what my life would be like single."

"That's true, you wouldn't have any responsibilities. You

could spend money how you want without checking in, and you could come out and party anytime without feeling guilty," Lucy said in agreement.

I watched as three men approached their table, and soon they were all drinking together and laughing. A certain amount of dread began to fill me as I saw Blakely growing closer to one of the guys. It seemed that personal space was about to be thrown out the window. I kept watch as the girls drank more, and soon they were beyond their tolerance and became inebriated.

I watched as the boys helped the girls up and walked them out of the bar. I followed tearfully behind as they entered a hotel. I froze when I got off the elevator and watched Blakely enter a hotel room with one of the men.

"Aubrey, I know this is painful. It reminds you of your ex's affair as well. We don't need to stay to know what sin is happening. I want to jump ahead two months and go back to their kitchen."

I nodded silently, in agreement with the Holy Spirit.

I found myself Philip-Transported back into their kitchen. Nick was standing at the sink washing dishes. Again I heard his phone ringing, and once again Nick put the phone on speaker.

"Hello."

"Hey, I am running a few minutes late, but will be there shortly. Do you have a few minutes that we could talk?"

"Sure."

Nick quietly finished putting away the dishes and made his way into the dining room. He absentmindedly looked through the bay window to the neighbor's house. Soon he heard the front door open. Blakely tentatively made her way into the dining room.

Nick waited for her to begin. A part of him dreaded what was coming. Ever since two months ago when Blakely hadn't come home until the next morning, she had grown more and more distant.

Blakely looked at Nick, wondering how to begin this conversation. The last two months had been filled with one argument after another, and she dreaded what his reaction would be to her news.

"Nick, I'm pregnant."

Nick froze. This was not what he was expecting to hear, especially because they hadn't been intimate for four months. Understanding dawned, and dread filled Nick's eyes.

"Blakely, you didn't stay faithful?" The question came out filled with pain.

Blakely guiltily looked away. "I didn't mean to. I got super drunk two months ago, and it wasn't until I woke up at the hotel room with a guy from the night before that the reality hit me. I honestly don't even remember that night, I blacked out so hard, but the evidence is in my womb now." Tears began to stream from Blakely's eyes as the reality of her situation hit her.

She had gone from telling her friends she couldn't wait to get divorced and be single, to finding out that she was going to be a mother. The fear of what Nick would decide to do filled her with dread. She wasn't ready to do this alone. She looked at Nick again to find tears falling down his face as he stared at her in shock.

Sadness filled me as I watched them. It was obvious their relationship would never be the same again. The betrayal and her lack of repentance hit hard. All I heard from her words is that it was the beer's fault, that it was because she was drunk. I shook my head, filled with deep sadness.

I took a long breath and in the next second found myself Philip-Transported to a business office.

Chapter 27

I looked around the room and realized I was in a lawyer's office. There were law books, codes, and guidelines on the bookshelf, paperwork neatly stacked on the desk, and it was obviously a slow day. Finally, two men entered and I silently observed the situation.

"Robert, we have lost a couple of big clients recently. I'm working on bringing in some new clients, but until then we are going to have to move you to a thirty-hour weekly schedule."

Robert nodded. Truth be told, he had been expecting this news since the clients left last month. Robert watched his boss walk out and began to think about all the financial needs his family had this month. His oldest son needed money for football, and his youngest daughter needed money for dance lessons and all that went with that. Robert rubbed his eyes in frustration and sat back in his chair.

Robert had dark brown hair, and his features showed his father's Thailand roots, but his lighter tan skin came from his mother, who was Caucasian European.

He and his wife, Nicole, had been married for seventeen years. He had always worked hard to provide for his family, and took great pride in the fact that his work allowed his wife to be a stay-at-home mom. Robert began to crunch the numbers and figure out how this pay cut would affect his family needs.

Silently, I observed Robert go over the numbers. I saw the frustration building inside of him, as the numbers weren't matching up.

"Aubrey, we have seen the root cause of a problem that is about to explode. I want you to observe two months down the road now."

I nodded, and suddenly I was Philip-Transported to a football field. There was no breeze, and the sun's rays rapidly heated my face. Sweat began to drip from my forehead and I pulled out my hair tie to grab all the baby hairs again. To my surprise my hair was blonde now, not blue. I looked around as the shouting caught my attention, and tugged my hair back up into a ponytail.

I noticed Robert right away, as he was yelling the loudest for his son on the field. I made my way over to observe him and his family. Nicole was shouting just as loud as Robert. Their son Tim had just made a touchdown and they were all jumping for joy. The past couple of months had been trying for the family. Robert had grown increasingly agitated with the kids, and his patience level seemed to have withered as well. It felt good to have time to laugh and scream with joy instead of frustration.

Nicole looked down at their young daughter, Jen, who was jumping alongside them. Nicole sighed. She knew Robert had been under a lot of pressure since his hours were cut at work. She had started looking for a job this week even though she knew Robert was against it. But she really wanted to help relieve the pressure and give them some breathing room financially.

I watched as the family headed to their car after the game. As I watched them go, I was transferred forward in time to the family's back deck, where Nicole and Robert were sitting, enjoying the outdoors.

Nicole was figuring out how to approach this topic. She knew Robert would not be a fan, but at this point it was important for Nicole to show him that they could do this together, that she had his back, and together, they could overcome this financial difficulty.

"How are you feeling about your work hours? Has your boss mentioned when they will be switching it back to full-time?"

Robert sighed and rubbed his eyes. "Not yet. He said in a couple of months a few big clients will be joining, so we just need to get through maybe five or six months. Then everything will go back to normal."

Nicole nodded. "That's great news, dear. You know I really want to support you during this time. I….I was able to find a part-time job. It's seasonal and will only be for three months, but I thought it would be a great help for you."

"*No*! I already told you that I don't want you working! I am the man of this family and I am the provider. All you need to do is sit back and let me do my thing. I don't need your help."

"But Robert, I could at least help relieve some of the financial strain for a couple months. Then you would only need to stress about two months."

"*Nicole*! Did you not hear me? I do not need your support or help. I have got this. I will figure it out. You just focus on the kids and run this house. I am a man and I don't need a woman's help."

Nicole sat back in surprise. She always knew Robert had a chauvinistic attitude towards women, but she thought that eventually he would see her worth and value and recognize how her talents and skills complimented his.

Nicole had never wanted to be the wife that sat back and made the husband do everything for her. She had always wanted a relationship where she could stand side by side with her husband, sheltered safely under his arm, and yet a support. But right now Robert made her feel as if she was a burden and had nothing to offer him.

Nicole closed her eyes in pain. She had given up her job as a nurse when they had gotten married, even though she loved her job and helping others. But she knew with starting a family that she wanted to be more hands-on with her children. Now that they were getting older, she had always imagined going back to work and being able to help her husband with the burden of finances. Not take it all on, because that would be too much, but even just adding a little cushion was better than nothing.

But now it looked like Robert would never agree to her going back to work. He wouldn't agree with her dream, and no matter what situation they faced, he would never let her stand with him.

Robert was trying to calm himself down. There was no way he would let his wife work. He didn't need a woman helping him or taking credit for their financial freedom. No, Nicole just needed to stay at home and do her part of watching the kids. He would take care of the rest. So what if it was stressful and caused him to treat his family harshly? They could just have compassion and understanding for him and when his job went back to normal, then he would too.

Nicole leaned back silently, knowing it was pointless to continue this fight.

I watched, surprised at Robert's attitude, which clearly said he didn't need or want his wife's help.

"Holy Spirit, he is missing out on a great opportunity of walking through a trial together with his wife."

"Yes, yes he is."

I found myself Philip-Transported into a ranch-style home.

Chapter 28

I looked around at the open-floor plan of the ranch-style home. Although the interior design was beautiful, my eyes were drawn to the mess surrounding me. Toys were all over the place, laundry was in piles, and dishes were waiting to be cleaned. I made my way to the back room, one that was closed off from the rest of the space. It was a sunroom, and sitting in a chair, watching her kids play in the backyard, was a middle-aged women. She had ash-blonde curly hair, blue eyes, and her face held a look of pure exhaustion. I noticed five kids playing outside, ranging in age from four to ten. I began to observe her.

Hazel was exhausted. It had been a busy day so far with running kids to appointments, making them lunch, and now they were playing, but Hazel didn't have the energy to clean the house. She loved being a mother, but some days all the responsibilities that went with it were a bit overwhelming.

Hazel's phone began to buzz. As she looked down to see who was calling, a deep sigh broke from her lips.

"Hello."

"How were the kids' appointments?" Aiden asked.

"It was good. They are all ready for school next month."

"Great. I will be home on time today. Please make sure you have dinner ready at six pm."

"Sure, will do."

Hazel hung up the phone and knew she needed to get the house ready before her husband came home. She would never hear the end of it if it wasn't. Slowly she made her way out and began the work of cleaning up the toys and starting the laundry.

Soon it was time to prep for dinner and get the table ready. Hazel glanced at the clock and began rushing faster. No matter how many hours she worked, it seemed like it was never enough to keep up with the work at home.

At five-fifty-five sharp, I watched as a man walked in. He was tall at six feet, with blonde hair and eyes that were sharp and brown.

Aiden came through the door. "I'm home."

He looked around and noticed with annoyance there were still a couple of piles of laundry on the floor, not to mention some toys still strewn about. Aiden decided that he would have to talk to Hazel about it after dinner.

The kids, who had made their way indoors, glanced at their dad and started putting away their toys.

Hazel quickly placed the food on the table and had the kids wash up. They all hurried to sit down as Aiden made his way to the head of the table.

I watched silently as tension settled over the home. The children had all grown quiet and serious, and Hazel kept glancing at Aiden, especially when she noticed the two piles of laundry she hadn't gotten to yet. Dread filled her, but she continued to put food on the kids' plates.

The children ate quietly as Aiden and Hazel made small talk.

Soon dinner was over and the kids began their evening night activities, which were cleaning their rooms, reading, and then finally going to bed. Hazel helped the younger two with their activities, and checked in with the older kids making sure everything was done correctly. Once the kids were reading, she put another load of clothes in, and then she went to the kitchen and began washing the dishes.

Aiden sat in his reclining chair in the living room, watching the news on TV.

As I watched the couple, I saw Hazel finish the dishes and put them away, clean up the rest of toys, complete the laundry, get the kids ready for bed and then into bed, and finally, I saw as she brought her husband a cup of hot tea and sat down on the couch.

"How was your day?" Hazel asked quietly.

"It was good. I finished a big design job, and the client was impressed with it. This weekend I invited my client and his wife over, so you will need to make sure the house is clean and plan a good meal for them."

Hazel nodded, immediately thinking about the kids' activities this weekend for sports practice or games, and started planning out how to get it all done.

"Hazel, why weren't you able to get the house completely finished today? You had all day to get everything done the way I like. What did you do today, sit and relax?"

Hazel sighed. She had been waiting for Aiden to bring this up. When they had first gotten married, Aiden had told her that his responsibilities would be working and providing for them and her responsibilities would be paying bills, cooking and cleaning, and taking care of the kids. At the time, Hazel thought that was a good idea and didn't have a problem with it. She had assumed that Aiden would help when needed and that she would be given some time to relax. However, when their first child came she realized that wouldn't be the case.

When the baby would cry at night she still had to get up and feed and do diapers. She had to learn how to keep house and be a mom without help. As more kids came, and she eventually had twins, Hazel had reached her end. She was exhausted and honestly just wanted her husband to help her, instead of watching TV and ignoring her and the children.

She had recently shared this with a best friend, and had become discouraged after hearing about her marriage. Her friend Elizabeth had told her how her husband would come home from work and play with the kids. He would help bring food to the table, feed the kids, help with the dishes and cleaning the house, etc. At the very beginning of the marriage he had told her that he knew it was hard to raise kids and keep the home, and he wanted to help bear the weight with her. So they would turn it into a time of fun. Sometimes they would play their favorite oldies music, sometimes they would tease or just have the adult conversation that she missed when she was with the kids. Her husband would always make it a fun and enjoyable time, instead of pressuring her—or working in annoyance.

Hazel had noticed what she was missing out on. For ten years it had been she who raised the children, went to every game, activity, or appointment. It was she who took care of the housework, and she missed having loving and deep conversations with her husband. It saddened her that the idea of being with her and helping her didn't even cross his mind. In fact, the idea of doing any of it caused him to become harsh and annoyed with her. So to keep the peace, she quit asking for help, and eventually they didn't have much to talk about.

Hazel looked over at Aiden, who was once again engrossed in his phone. With tears in her eyes, she quietly went to get ready for bed. Aiden didn't even notice she was gone until an hour later when he got up to get ready for bed himself.

Suddenly I was Philip-Transported to a residential garage.

Chapter 29

I was quite surprised to find myself in a garage. It was a bit messy. There were tools lying around, and it looked like it was being reorganized before winter. I watched as a man came in, and I silently watched him.

Calvin was a hard-working, middle-class, blue-collar worker. He loved working with his hands and creating furniture, toys, and more for others. It was a hobby of his that had started when he was a young lad and his father and grandfather taught him the tricks of the trade. After graduating from college, he had decided to make it his full-time job, because everyone loved his custom pieces.

Calvin was getting to be in his mid-forties, and he had reddish-brown hair, blue eyes, and tan skin, and his hands were calloused from hard work. Lately, he had been swamped with orders, and he had been working longer hours to get them all completed. Owning a small business was not for a faint of heart. As the owner, designer, and creator of the pieces, Calvin put in long hours every day.

He and his wife, Willow had been married for twenty years. They had a couple of kids who were both out of the house.

"Calvin, are you done for the day?"

Calvin looked over at Willow standing the doorway. Today she was dressed to go out with friends. Her red ringlets were styled just right, her hazel eyes had a questioning look, and her fair skin shown bright in the darkly lit garage.

"Not yet, dear. Are you about to go out?"

"Yes, but I have a huge list of things that I need you to have done by tomorrow."

Calvin raised his eyebrows. Now that Willow was working from home too, it had changed the flow of their relationship.

Before, Calvin could go in the garage and work on his orders without interference or feeling obligated to fulfill his wife's list of chores. But now with Willow home every day, there was frustration and constant distractions.

"Okay, but I have a large order that needs to be filled this week, so some of these items may need to wait till next week."

"*No*! I want them done this week! Honestly, I have been asking you for four months to finish painting the guest bathroom and get the lighting fixed and ready. I want to invite some guests next month and the bathroom needs to be finished."

"Honey, I understand, but that means I have a month to get it done. Please be patient."

Willow rolled her eyes. "I need to go, but I expect for the items on the list to be done when I get back."

I watched as Willow left and Calvin again went back to work getting his garage organized so he could begin preparing the next order. He didn't stop once to rest, but continued to work hard the three hours till his wife got home.

"Have you seriously done nothing on my list?" Willow screamed. Her frustration was mounting. All Calvin did was work on orders, and it irritated her that he couldn't make time to get the things on her list done. No matter how many times she told him, he still wouldn't do it when she wanted it done.

Was it really that hard to get it done when she asked for it?

"Willow, I have talked to you about this before. From 7am-6pm and an hour for lunch break are my working hours. I will not work on any chore from your list, unless I have no orders that need to be made. In the evenings and weekends, I try hard to complete your lists, but they have become increasingly harder to do, because there is way too much. Also, most of them are wants that don't need to happen right this instant, and I think we need to rearrange the list to prioritize what is most important for right now."

"*No!* It's all important. I don't understand why you can't just get things done when I ask. You could always work on your job stuff in the evenings when you are done with my list."

"Willow, it doesn't work that way. This business is important and I need to keep a routine so I don't get behind on orders."

"I guess I'm just not that important to you, Calvin. If you really cared about me then you would get the stuff done when I ask."

Willow stormed off and slammed the door. Calvin watched her go and sighed deeply. His patience was beginning to wear thin. He looked at her list again.

To DO LIST:

1. *Paint guest bathroom*

2. *Put in new lights*

3. *Vacuum house*

4. *Organize the freezer and the pantry*

5. *Pull weeds in landscape*

6. *Wash car*

7. *Fix cupboard in kitchen*

8. *Wash kitchen floors*

9. *Clean bathrooms*

10. *Wash windows*

Calvin sighed again. Willow had always had to-do lists, and she would nag at him till they were accomplished, but in the last couple of years it had grown worse.

Once six pm and after Calvin had dinner, he started on Willow's list. He vacuumed the floors, washed the kitchen floors, and even got the bathrooms cleaned. But he knew that still wouldn't make Willow happy.

"Honey, can you mark off the list 'vacuum, wash kitchen floor, and clean bathrooms'?"

"Well…at least you got three things off the list done. I wonder if you can finish the rest before another four months go by."

"Willow, I'm sorry I can't get your list done right when you want it, but it's important for you to recognize my job too, and that I am also working hard to provide for our family."

"Sorry, it's all my fault. I should stop expecting you to have things done when I ask you to. I'm sorry you think I'm unrealistic with my list. Lists are what I do, and this is who I am so…"

Calvin shook his head, because all he heard was, 'sure it's all my fault. Obviously you are not able to meet my deadlines, but I am going to make you feel bad for it. You just don't love me for who I am and this is who I am, and I won't change.' Except, none of that was how he really felt about Willow.

Suddenly I was Philip-Transported back to the quiet, peaceful, and secluded beach boasting the brilliant ocean view.

Chapter 30

"Holy Spirit, some of those were really hard to observe, and others just made me uncomfortable."

"Yes, there was a lot to observe, and some things were so hidden that most people would think nothing of them."

"Hmmm...I can see that."

"So let's talk about the five observations you just observed."

"Sounds good, Holy Spirit. The first observation hit too close to home. I remember how my ex-husband teased me about a girl kissing him while we were dating. I remember arguments when he would make sarcastic comments about abandoning me, and the multiple times he threw out the word '*divorce*'.

"I have noticed more and more of these so-called pranks and it really disgusts me, because those who pull them are completely clueless that they are destroying their relationships and soon the spouse will no longer trust anything they say. They will always wonder if it is a joke, or if, for once, they are being serious. It's a horrible way to live, and it really destroys the relationship.

"'*Divorce*' should never be discussed, spoken, or even mentioned in a marriage. Too many believers throw the word around like it's nothing, but it's a big word to the Father. The Father does not desire anyone to divorce. He granted it, for specific reasons, but believers today get married and in the back of their mind they think to themselves, 'it's okay, if it doesn't work out we will just get a divorce.' The divorce rate amongst believers is staggering. Now if the spouse and kids are being abused (emotionally, physically, sexually, and/or spiritually) by the other spouse, then they need to get away from the marriage and divorce. If the other partner is not being faithful, and the Lord leads the spouse to divorce, then so be it. But if the individual just wants to divorce because they are no longer in love, or marriage is hard, etc., then divorce is the easy way out and not what God intended.

"Too many believers take the covenant of marriage and cheapen it. Honestly, my heart broke for Nick. I know so many couples where the wife or husband began to live apart from the Father. Their choices became more and more worldly until they completely left the marriage. They didn't remain faithful to the Father nor to the spouse. I also find it extremely sad how many couples put themselves in compromising situations with someone of the opposite sex when they are married.

"When someone is dating, engaged, and married, they should not be doing one-on-one things with the opposite sex. They should not be flirty or ignoring boundaries. Blakely's whole excuse about being drunk triggered my post-traumatic stress disorder. No one should ever put themselves in a situation where they are not clear-minded around the opposite sex. The Father's children should be held to higher accountability than what they are. Sin should be called sin. Believers should be taught about repentance and turning away from sin.

"Experiencing the effects of an affair and the betrayal and how it became part of the trauma affecting my post-traumatic stress disorder showed me why the Father calls His children to be faithful to their marriage bed."

"You are right, Aubrey. So many take the covenant of marriage as a joke, and they don't understand that when they get married, the Father has joined them together as one. Two become one. The pranking and jokes, throwing the word '*divorce*' around are just a few of the ways believers treat their marriages as something other than sacred. Their hearts reveal contempt for the other person, and they find enjoyment at the suffering of the one they are supposed to be protecting.

"So many of these are heart issues. They have forgotten to put the other person first, to love them as they would want to be loved, and to respect each other as the Father's sons and daughters. Once they won their spouse's heart, they quit running after their heart."

"I never thought about it that way before, but it makes sense. Once they got the person's heart they became self-focused again, intent on meeting their own needs instead of their spouse's.

"Robert and Nicole's story was very sad. All she wanted was to meet her spouse's need by being a support for him. To stand shoulder to shoulder, holding each other up. Not only did her husband refuse, but he didn't even ask the Father what calling, ministry, and purpose He had given his wife. Instead, he made the decision and chose to keep her from being obedient to the Father."

"You are right, Aubrey. A husband should be praying about his wife's purpose, and even his kids', and then he should be their biggest supporter of what the Father has put in their hearts. Yet, how many husbands forget this responsibility? They forget that the wife still has a calling upon her life. How many husbands, when they reach heaven, will hear the Father say, 'you did this part right in your marriage, however, you failed to help your wife bring My Kingdom to the world'? Just as wives have a purpose and calling, so do husbands. It is just as important for wives to help their husbands reach their full potential in calling and ministry. We will talk about this more later, but it's something to keep in mind for now."

"Sounds good, Holy Spirt. I also find it interesting that there is the negative aspect where the husband refuses to work and provide for his family, and instead does nothing but sit at home. He expects the wife to do all the work and provide financially, while he can sit back and be lazy. Both are wrong. Neither one are loving options. Marriage is meant to be a healthy balance of supporting the wife, and helping her to rise to her calling.

"Hazel's story made me sad too. I was in the same situation, where the responsibilities of the family were placed solely on my shoulders and my ex-husband had no real desire to help me. Any time I asked, he made it known he did not appreciate going out of his way to help. I wanted to cry when I learned about Hazel's friend, whose husband made it a point to help his wife. Not only that, but he purposefully made it fun. He put in the effort to make it a time of intimacy, a time of growing together, something that they could do and enjoy. He made it special. Why do responsibilities have to be so hard and overwhelming? It makes complete sense that they can actually be beautiful, playful, and intimate connections with each other. I wish more couples made responsibilities fruitful and pleasurable experiences.

"Finally, in the last observation we watched as someone put their own wants and desires first, without understanding the other person. There was no compassion for the other person's work, and I thought it was sad that she used manipulation to try to get her husband to agree to her way. She used guilt to make him feel like he wasn't doing enough. She forgot to be thankful for all that he was doing right. I understand, Holy Spirit, why You said, 'It's all heart issues.' All of this comes down to their heart. They put themselves first and they do not use the fruit of the spirit, they love themselves more than their spouse, they are prideful, and the list goes on and on. Basically, they are choosing the flesh and sin over the Father and their spirit."

"Isn't it amazing how simple all this is, Aubrey? Everything falls into two categories: flesh or spirit, satan or the Father. Believers blame their failed relationship on the other party without looking at their own faults and wrongs."

"I agree with that. When the Father had me writing Beyond Held Hostage, it was a time when He and I went into my own point of view, my own flaws and mistakes, and the shifts in perspective that I needed to make so my future would not be a repeat of the past. I think it also shows that many believers are not sensitive to Your voice and leading. If they were, they would recognize when they are in the flesh and in the wrong, and they would get themselves back into alignment with truth."

"Simple, and yet the hardest thing for people to do is surrender to the Father and listen to Me. Aubrey, would you like to hear what happened with Nick and Blakely?"

"Yes, Holy Spirit. I would like to know what happened."

"Nick took a couple of months to work through the betrayal, and he and Blakely started counseling together. Nick came to an understanding that this baby needed him as a father, and after the Father asked him if he would say yes to Him, Nick chose to take the child as his own. He learned how to walk in forgiveness towards Blakely, and soon things started to get better between them.

"After the nine months, Blakely gave birth to a healthy baby girl, and Nick loved her as if she was his own. He took the responsibility of fatherhood as the most important decision he had made. However, two months after the baby girl was born, Blakely decided motherhood and wifehood weren't what she wanted anymore. They ended up getting a divorce, and full custody of the child went to Nick. Nick pressed into the Father and allowed Him to heal his heart, and while healing, he was an amazing father to his daughter. Later on, the Father would bring a wife who would be everything this father and daughter would need."

"I am sad that Blakely didn't repent and change her ways, but I also love hearing about Nick's decision, and the fact that he raised his daughter as if she was truly his. The fact is, she is his. She is absolutely his daughter, and the fact that he chose her makes it that much more powerful. She is chosen, she is wanted, she is loved, and her daddy is giving her an amazing example of our Father."

"Aubrey, it's time to witnesses the new blueprints the Father has. Are you ready?"

"I am ready."

"Three of the married couples you will see are actually some of those you met during the witnessing part of dating and engaged journey. The Father wanted you to see the fulfillment of their beautiful stories."

I smiled with joy at the thought of seeing these wonderful couples, now married and walking out the blueprints that the Father has.

Suddenly I was Philip-Transported to an outdoor gun range.

Chapter 31

I looked around with surprise, but also excitement. Recently the Father had led me to start learning how to protect myself, so I felt very comfortable in this loud setting. The sun was high in sky, beating down on my head. A gentle breeze cooled my face. To my right, were wooden frames with targets stapled on. Wooden posts on the range's sidelines showed the distance in foot measurements. I turned to the left to face the gunmen and women. I moved closer when I noticed one couple in particular enjoying each other's company, and shooting a 9mm Glock. I smiled wider as I drew closer to Anastasia and Ethan.

"Good job, Anastasia. You're really getting the hang of it." Ethan smiled with admiration at his beautiful bride.

"Aubrey, I want you to listen to what Ethan is thinking about. Their marriage started off bumpy even though they had so much going for them, because every marriage will have struggles as each couple learns how to apply the Father's blueprints to it."

I nodded and listened in.

They had been married for eight months and God had been taking them through a time of really learning to understand one another's hearts. Ethan thought back to their second month of being married. During that time, Anastasia was getting used to being a wife, and starting to understand the importance of not jumping ahead in her independence, but learning how to rely on him. It had been a challenging time for them that month. Anastasia had her own views and ways of doing things that weren't necessarily wrong, but didn't allow Ethan to be included as the husband.

Ethan remembered how, at the beginning of the third month of marriage, it boiled over to the point that he had to confront her. Anastasia had decided that for Christmas they would be going to her family's. Not that Ethan didn't mind, but his family and their traditions were important too. Ethan had wanted to talk about it and come up with a plan where both could have time with their families together for Christmas. He understood that Anastasia's family usually did things on both Christmas Eve and Christmas Day, but now that they were a couple it was important to become one.

Ethan remembered how he had gently explained it to his wife. "Anastasia, sweetie, I understand that you want to continue your family traditions for the holidays, but we are married now. There's two of us. It hurt me that you didn't think about me and see the importance of including my family into our marriage."

He remembered how Anastasia had grown defensive. Her response had not been honoring.

"Shouldn't you be loving to me? Putting me first? This is important to me and I don't want it to change."

"Sweetie, our marriage goes both ways. I have never wanted our marriage to be one-sided, where just one person's needs are being met. That isn't healthy, nor is it what God designed for marriages. He desires that both individuals love and honor one another, and meet each other's physical and emotional needs. Honor is always given, meaning we treat one another highly and with great esteem and devotion, and as God's valuable children. Respect, however, is earned. I try very hard through my actions and the way that I love you to show you respect and earn your respect in turn.

"Ignoring my feelings and not even taking them into consideration is not honoring or respectful, sweetie. I work to be diligent in honoring and respecting you as my wife. I consider your feelings and emotions, and I make decisions for what will be best for you. So even challenging you in this is a way for me to do what is best for you."

Anastasia had walked away angry, but later that day, after she had spent time with her spiritual mother, she came back to apologize.

"Honey, I want to apologize to you. You were right. I wasn't being loving when I ignored your heart. My response to your correction wasn't honoring or respectful. I am really sorry. I want to grow in this area. I don't want our marriage to be all about me, and in the process cause you to lose yourself. I married you for who you are right now, and I want to keep you that way. It was wrong of me to assume we would just cater to my family and to me. It also showed lack of love towards your family. Please forgive me, honey?"

"I forgive you, sweetie." Ethan had smiled with joy at his beautiful wife. "What got you thinking about this?"

"Well, my friend started telling me about her first marriage. She had made her husband give way to her, and eventually he left her because the marriage became one-sided. If she didn't get her way she would manipulate him, guilt-trip him, and even became disrespectful in front of her family or their friends. It destroyed their marriage, and when she met her new husband, they had a long talk about her attitude and selfishness before he would even consider marriage. My friend also shared the verses that really impacted her decision in it. Ephesians 5:21-28 (NIV) says, '[21] Submit to one another out of reverence for Christ. [22] Wives, submit yourselves to your own husbands as you do to the Lord. [23] For the husband is the head of the wife as Christ is the head of the church, his body, of which he is the Savior. [24] Now as the church submits to Christ, so also wives should submit to their husbands in everything. [25] Husbands, love your wives, just as Christ loved the church and gave himself up for her [26] to make her holy, cleansing her by the washing with water through the word, [27] and to present her to himself as a radiant church, without stain or wrinkle or any other blemish, but holy and blameless. [28] In this same way, husbands ought to love their wives as their own bodies. He who loves his wife loves himself.'

"As she read me the verses, I was really convicted. You realized that my selfishness goes against God's character and you lovingly corrected me in it. I realized that it was wrong of me. God doesn't want me to be selfish, only considering myself. He wants us to put each other first, because then we will meet each other's needs and accept the love we are showing each other."

Ethan had nodded his head with approval, because he knew his wife was getting it right. She understood that to love one another meant that instead of draining the life from the other person, each purposefully looked for ways to fill the other back up. Instead of nagging at each other, or forcing a spouse to chose one family over another and lose everything, it was important that they continued to fill each other up with love and encouragement, and, most importantly, allowed each other to have a voice. It was important for their hearts to be heard.

"I love you so very much, sweetie. Thank you for taking my correction and for understanding my heart as well. Are you okay if we talk about Christmas plans, and how we can become one family?"

"I would love to, honey."

I watched their beautiful conversation take place, and I realized that my own longing for this deep, gentle communication was growing within me.

Chapter 32

With a smile on my face, I was quickly Philip-Transported to a backyard. The breeze came up from behind and I watched as my dress billowed in front of me, and I was amazed anew that my hair was blonde. Although my curiosity was piqued, I didn't have time to think about it. For before me, was a large backyard, with a beautiful landscape tracing the outskirts. I watched as Jeremiah and Emily made their way outside to where I stood. I was filled with joy at how much in love they still were.

It had been a year since Jeremiah and Emily had married. They had worked hard to fight for the marriage that they both longed for and felt honored God.

"Ems, I asked you to help me, why do you always make things harder for me?"

Jeremiah was beginning to grow annoyed with Emily. He had asked her to weed the landscape while he mowed, but instead of throwing the weeds in a bucket, she had tossed them onto the grass that he was about to mow.

Jeremiah didn't want to lose his cool with his wife, so he walked away and started putting the weeds in the bucket.

Emily stood silently, her eyes troubled and worried.

"Aubrey, I am going to open your ears to hear their thought processes, and to give understanding to their perspectives, and how they shift."

"Okay, Holy Spirit." I began to listen intently.

Emily sighed as she watched Jeremiah pick up the weeds. A fear was beginning to tug at her heart. This situation felt so similar to her past boyfriend. Emily had thought that Justin was a great boyfriend, but as the months went by he began to gaslight her, making her believe that everything was her fault, and causing her to question her own mind and thoughts. She began to wonder if she was seeing him correctly. When a friend told her that gaslighting her and giving her the silent treatment was abuse, she began to recognize how she had changed. She had quickly broken up with him and had worked hard to heal, overcome the pain, and work through her responses to similar situations.

Watching Jeremiah ignore her and pick up the weeds in frustration was triggering to her. She was starting to fear that he would become the same, even though she knew he wasn't. She knew Jeremiah's character well. She knew his heart. But at this moment, all of that was pushed out of her mind as the fear reared high.

Silently, she prayed, 'God, I don't want to see Jeremiah through the lens of Justin. He isn't Justin. His heart is not the same, his views are not the same, and his character is not the same. Help me to overcome this fear that is being triggered within me, and help me to see Jeremiah the way You see him.'

I watched as Emily tentatively made her way to Jeremiah.

"Um…honey, could we talk for a minute?"

Jeremiah glanced at Emily and immediately recognized that something was wrong. Taking a deep breath, he calmed himself. "Sure, Ems, what's up?"

"I know that you love me. I know that you care about me, but I have to be honest…your response to me back there was triggering for me. It brought up all the fears from my past relationship to the forefront, and I don't want to think of you that way. I want to see you through God's eyes."

Jeremiah's heart broke. He never meant to hurt her. In fact, he was trying not to hurt her with his anger, so he had remained silent, but it was silence that her past boyfriend had used against her. All the anger and frustration that Jeremiah had been feeling left as compassion rippled through his heart.

"Oh, Ems, pumpkin, I didn't mean for my silence to hurt you.

I was angry and frustrated, and I didn't want to respond out of that so I chose to stay quiet. I didn't intend to use that silence as a weapon against you, I was choosing to be quiet and talk with God so I could walk in love and instead of the flesh."

Emily nodded in relief as Jeremiah explained his thought process and heart. Her fears began to melt away, and she could breathe again.

Jeremiah wrapped her in his embrace. "I know your past relationship was hard. We've worked together to overcome these triggers and to have healthier responses between us. I am sorry for hurting you, pumpkin. Even though it wasn't my intention, my choice of silence hurt you. That wasn't loving towards you. Please forgive me?"

"I forgive you. Please forgive me too, I should have thought through the weed pulling. I should have realized I was making things harder for you. That wasn't caring or loving on my part either. Please forgive me, honey?"

"I forgive you. Let's pray, pumpkin."

Emily nodded in agreement.

I watched them bow their heads and hold each other in a tight embrace. I listened as Jeremiah led them in a prayer of repentance and for wisdom in navigating past traumas and fears. It was so very beautiful to witness the Father's joy and delight over the love His children displayed.

"Holy Spirit, they are giving the blueprints to Colossians 3:12-14 (NIV) which says, '[12] Therefore, as God's chosen people, holy and dearly loved, clothe yourselves with compassion, kindness, humility, gentleness and patience. [13] Bear with each other and forgive one another if any of you has a grievance against someone. Forgive as the Lord forgave you. [14] And over all these virtues put on love, which binds them all together in perfect unity.'

"They are demonstrating how our perspectives are, for the most part, not based on actual reality. When we look from our own perspective, we miss so much information, and it shows that we truly need the Father's perspective to be activated in our lives. We need to see each other through His eyes, and have hearts that are quick to sense the conviction that comes from You. John 16:8 (NIV) says, '8 When he comes, he will prove the world to be in the wrong about sin and righteousness and judgment…'

"Holy Spirit, they are letting You lead them in loving one another. They are giving You room to move and work and aren't keeping their hearts hardened towards each other."

"Aubrey, when married couples let Me lead, I am able to bring redemption and healing into every area of their marriage."

With that, I was Philip-Transported to a women's domestic violence center.

Chapter 33

I looked around at my surroundings and saw the hurting women gathered around a woman who looked very familiar. I made my way closer and saw that it was Adelyn. She was speaking and sharing the Father's love with the women who had experienced abuse from the ones meant to protect them. I silently witnessed as she let the Holy Spirit flow from her.

"I know that many of you are questioning your worth and value, and wonder what the Father could possibly have for your future. I want to encourage you that He has a plan for you, but even more important than that is His desire for deep covenant relationship with you. You see, He longs to restore you, heal you, and realign you. You do not need to remain a victim or live in survivor mode. Instead you can fully thrive out of relationship with the Father. As you begin to break through the memories and trauma and the Father takes you deeper into relationship with Him, you will find that the one who hurt you will no longer have power over you. You will be walking in full authority given to you by the Father." Adelyn continued to speak over the women and after she was done, she began to pray over them. The presence of the Father fell upon the room, and in that intimate atmosphere, the ladies began to draw close to the Father, receiving healing, freedom, and breakthrough, and many recommitted their relationship with the Father.

I was so immersed in the Father's presence that it took some minutes to realize that the Holy Spirit had taken me to another location. In surprise I realized that I was in Kenya, at an orphanage. The unforgiving heat was the first thing I noticed. I took a minute to adjust to the heat and humidity. Surrounding me were five, cement block one-story buildings with tin roofs, and standing before me were beautiful Kenyan children ranging in age from two to eighteen. Playing amongst them were five Korean-Caucasian kids. The oldest child was a boy of eight. Next were two sets of twins; the first set were five-year-old girls, and the last set were a two-year-old boy and girl.

I drew close and watched as the children mingled together, playing and laughing with the Kenyan children. You could see their genuine love for each other, the way that they showed honor and respect to each other as siblings, and to the other children. I sensed the Holy Spirit in them, and I was curious who the children belonged to.

Soon I noticed a group of Kenyan adults walking toward the kids, followed by a couple that was very familiar. Adelyn and Do-Yun stood before me, and in that moment I could feel the anointing from the Father flowing from them. I moved to follow them.

"Kids, it's time to head into the bush to share the Gospel."

Do-Yun encouraged the children to quickly get ready. He loaded them up in the Jeep and soon they were on their way. After a couple hours of travel through dusty trails and extreme heat, they finally reached their location. In 2007 and 2012, Kenya had experienced a storm of violence after their elections. Many women were raped, and other sexual violence had taken place. Several men and women were killed, and others became homeless. Today, Adelyn and Do-Yun, along with their children, were going to go minister to some of the survivors. They were going to bring the good news of the Father, Yeshua, and the Holy Spirit.

A large group gathered together under an Aningeria adolfi-friederici tree. They all sat down together to listen to Do-Yun and Adelyn speak. Their translator stayed close beside them.

Do-Yun began to share his heart and speak the words the Holy Spirit had given him to say, while Adelyn began to pray in the Spirit.

"The Father knows what you have experienced, and He knows the pain that you have endured, as well as the loss of family and friends. Some of you are still living in the horror of those times, unable to move forward. The Father desires a relationship with you. At the very beginning of earth's time, He created us in His image. He formed each of us in our mother's womb, and He knows us all by name. Yet the ones He created first, turned away from Him and sinned against Him, bringing sin and darkness into the earth. Because of their choices, we now experience pain, death, sickness, and so much more.

"But the Father refused to leave us in this state. He promised that He would send His Son to come and overcome satan and his demons once and for all. Yeshua came as promised. He came to restore our relationship to the Father, so He laid down His very life in a horrible, painful death. He was crucified on a tree, and as He breathed His last He knew this was just the beginning. Because after three days, He rose again and after a time, He returned to heaven. But the Father promised that He wouldn't leave His children here alone. So He sent the Holy Spirit, who reveals the Father's heart to us, and through Him we are given insight, direction, and understanding.

"The Father is still not done with His promises, though. He longs that we be with Him in heaven, which is our true home, and so He will once again send His Son, Yeshua, to come for us. We will return with Him, and take our place in the Father's Kingdom.

"So while we are here on earth, experiencing the pain and suffering that is still connected to satan, we cling wholeheartedly to the Father. Through Him, we can have peace, healing, and freedom. Today, if you have not chosen the Father, if you have not accepted His Son, Yeshua, and if the Holy Spirit has not come to live inside of you, then choose Him today. Choose Him and let Him take you out of the past and into a future that is full of healing and joy. Choose to let Him move in your life and fill you with His love and presence."

As I watched Do-Yun preach and Adelyn pray in the Spirit, my eyes turned to their children, and I began to witness a beautiful sight. Their oldest son and the oldest set of twins were watching over the youngest twins. But as they took care of them they were also speaking in tongues and boldly praying forth the

Father's will. I was witnessing the power of a balanced family who were doing ministry together, and yet fully functioning as a family. The children were not suffering while the parents were ministering, but all together they were bringing the Father glory, loving each other, and walking in spirit. Tears flooded my eyes.

Do-Yun then led an altar call. A hundred men and women made their way forward for a personal relationship with the Father. I watched as Adelyn and the kids joined in praying over the new believers. They began to prophesy over them, healings began to take place, and I witnessed the power and gifts of the Holy Spirit activated. The tears would not stop falling down my face, and my heart was filled with the beauty I beheld.

Then in an instant, I was Philip-Transported to a church.

Chapter 34

I quickly fixed my hair, smoothing out the baby hairs that had escaped and checking my outfit to make sure I looked presentable for service. I looked around the sanctuary and admired its rustic design. There wasn't an abundance of pictures or added pieces to draw the eye. Instead the walls were walnut, framed with large windows, and the pews were made from logs. At the front of the sanctuary was a pulpit with a typical rectangular shape made from walnut, but the base was smaller and not as bulky. Behind the pulpit there was an altar made from the same wood, simple and elegant in design. Everywhere you looked was wood and windows. I looked outside and noticed the trees that surrounded the sanctuary, and up above a hint of blue peeked through the branches. It was a very quiet, calm, and serene atmosphere, and a sense of intimacy surrounded me.

"Holy Spirit, I can sense You so very strongly here. I can feel the Father's presence and how His glory hovers here."

"Yes Aubrey, this church has allowed Me room to move in their services and daily lives. Because they recognize Me and I am given all the space I need, the presence of the Father rests here. He fills this space with His anointing and power. This is a place where His bride comes carrying Me with them to be together in unity, worshiping the Father. Yeshua is glorified here. They keep the spiritual realm as the focus in all they do.

"Aubrey, there is a couple here I want you to witness, for they are going to reveal the Father's heart for both married couples and families. There are some very important things I want you to understand that you will need to grasp for your future."

"I understand. I will witness and if I run into anything

unknown, I will ask You."

With that I heard a couple entering the sanctuary. I turned to see a beautiful image of a family laughing together. The wife was very pregnant, as she was carrying twins, and there was such joy and delight in her face. Her dark brown, mono-lid eyes carried a wealth of wisdom and discernment. One look and I understood that she was able to read the seasons and times. She had long black hair and brown skin.

To her right was her husband, and he had ash-brown hair cut short, bold, piercing blue eyes, and pale skin. He stood a few inches taller than his wife. You could see that he loved to bring joy to others, and he enjoyed seeing the smiles of his wife and children.

Standing between them were triplets, two girls and one boy, and each one resembled a mix of their parents. They brought both the Korean and Caucasian look into one. Their skin was lighter than their mom's, and the boy had brown eyes while the girls had blue, but all three had dark brown hair. They were about three years old.

"I-Jun, darling, are you ready for your message?" Conroy asked his wife.

"Yes. The Holy Spirit has given me great inspiration. Are you ready with the music for worship, 여보 (pronounced yeo bo, meaning honey)?" I-Jun glanced at her children as she spoke to her husband.

"Yeah, I think we'll sing the three songs I showed you last night. After worship, depending on how the Holy Spirit leads, I'll turn it over to you for the message. The pastor talked to me yesterday and said they wanted us to take the lead today."

I-Jun nodded in agreement. "Not every church is willing to turn over their service to a guest speaker, but I believe the Father is going to honor them for their humility. They truly hold this church with hands opened wide to the Father."

Conroy nodded in agreement. As a family, they loved it when the Father brought them to churches like this one, where the pastors were humble and open for the Spirit to move. But they also recognized that even when the Father brought them to a church that wasn't like this, it was just as important, because that usually meant there were areas where the Father was going to use them to correct and bring the church back into realignment with truth (the Word).

"A-yeong, Chun-hee, Isaac, Mommy and Daddy will be leading worship together while you sit with Auntie. After worship you'll sit with Daddy while I give the message the Holy Spirit is leading me to share. I want you all to be listening and respectful. If the Father gives you something to share with the church, I want you to tell Daddy and he will give me a signal, understood?"

All three children nodded their heads and smiled, "Yes, Umma 음마 (mama)."

I sat in the first pew where I could both see the kids sitting with their auntie and watch I-Jun and Conroy on the platform. There was such an intimate atmosphere spreading through the room as I watched I-Jun and Conroy worship the Father. The presence of God swept through the sanctuary. I watched in awe as the children lifted their hands up to the Father and sang.

The gift of tongues began to spread throughout the building, and I heard as each child began to speak in tongues as well. I realized this was not foreign to them, and that even at such a young age the gifts of the Spirit were evident in their lives. Before the service was turned over to I-Jun, I watched as Isaac got his father's attention. Conroy approached his son, and together they talked. Conroy began to nod his head and then spoke into the microphone. "My son, Isaac, has been given a word from the Father and I want him to share."

My heart responded deeply as I listened to this child share one sentence. "Two equals one."

I took a deep breath. "Holy Spirit, does he mean me?"

"Yes, Aubrey, it's a word the Father wants you to know. 'Two equals one' means soon you will be married. You and your husband will become one, and together you will be a beautiful testament of the Father's power."

I nodded as tears trailed down my face.

Once again I was Philip-Transported to a hotel room. The blue circle-patterned carpet, dark blue walls, and white linens created an inviting feel to the space. There were two queen beds, a small table and chairs, and a couple of dressers.

I-Jun was sitting on one of the beds with A-yeong while Chun-hee and Isaac sat on the other. Conroy strolled into the hotel room.

"How's our daughter doing?" Conroy asked of I-Jun.

"Her temp still won't go down. You have an important meeting with the local pastors here. I am going to cancel my meeting with the women's shelter tonight and take care of her. I need to be here with her instead of asking your sister to watch her."

Conroy nodded his head. "I agree. We always said that our kids would be first in our ministry. Tomorrow I'll change my schedule around so that way you can still go to your meetings. Maybe see if they can change the meeting tonight to tomorrow?"

I-Jun nodded and quickly made the call.

I watched as Conroy left for his meeting, and I-Jun began to love on her kids. Although she looked tired, I watched her pour out her love on her kids. She held them, spoke lovingly to them, and all four cuddled together as I-Jun read them a story.

After a couple of hours, Conroy returned. He was tired from the meeting, but wanted to give I-Jun time to relax and fill up.

As I-Jun went to take a shower and relax, Conroy took over the nurturing role.

After a time, Chun-hee and Isaac began to argue with one another. Conroy lost his temper and shouted at them to be quiet. All three kids turned wide eyes to their father in surprise.

Conroy took a deep breath as regret filled him. He had worked hard not to follow in his father's footsteps of yelling at and being harsh with his kids. He had grown up with a father who constantly put him down and spoke negative words over him like, 'you never listen, get your act together.' He wanted to discipline them out of love, instead of letting frustration and anger take over. Conviction filled Conroy and he humbled himself before the Father.

"Chun-hee, Isaac, I'm so sorry that I yelled at you. That wasn't honoring of me. I came down harsh on you, and that wasn't necessary. Please forgive me?"

"We forgive you, A-ppa 아빠 (papa)," piped up Chun-hee and Isaac. They both turned to each other and smiled.

"I'm sorry, please forgive me for fighting with you?" They said to one another at the same time.

I was amazed at how Conroy walked out relationship, repentance, and obedience to the Father in front of his children. Not only did they learn what living for Yeshua was all about, but they learned how to follow their father's example and quickly made it right with one another. They were only three, and yet they understood how to walk in spirit instead of flesh. I watched as the three children cuddled up with their father, fully knowing they were loved and didn't need to fear him.

From there I was Philip-Transported to a condo in Seoul, South Korea. I found a mirror in the entryway of the condo and quickly checked my hair and make-up. The hallway was a deep forest green. I followed it until I reached an open-floor plan. There was a spacious living room to the right and to the left was the kitchen and dining room. The living room was full of blue and green accent pieces, representing the colors of the ocean. The wall behind the sofa was turquoise, decorated with a picture of the forest and a navy blue sofa, and the flooring was a deep walnut laminate. Toys were scattered on the ground. The kitchen had royal blue bottom cabinets, gray granite countertops, and walnut shelves for the upper cabinets. The backsplash was a blue, fish-scales pattern.

Conroy and the kids walked in. "Children, before your mother gets home from the store, I want you to clean the living room."

The kids got to work quickly. In ten minutes the place looked back to normal with each toy put back in its place.

I followed the kids as they made their way to their room and began to pick up their toys there. Soon Conroy joined them.

"Well done going above and beyond! Not only did you do an amazing job picking up what I asked you to, but you went even further than what I required and cleaned your room as well. Your mother is going to be very blessed when she sees this."

The kids glowed with pride and joy at their father's words.

Suddenly I was Philip-Transported back to my special beach.

Chapter 35

"Holy Spirit, why are we back here? Don't we have one more good relationship to witness?"

Laughter filled the Holy Spirit's voice as He spoke. "Yes, we do have one more. It is actually a continuation of I-Jun and Conroy's love story, but before we witness this next moment, I want to share with you how they dated."

"I would love to know more. They have such a deep connection with one another."

"They actually didn't know each other long. In fact, I started telling them about each other before they physically met. When the Father had Me bring them together, their connection was already deep and intimate, and they easily allowed Me access to their lives.

"Just as with Adelyn and Do-Yun, Conroy took the initiative to pursue I-Jun. They met, and two months later he began to pursue her, and a couple weeks later they became boyfriend and girlfriend. After two months of pursuing and being in a relationship, Conroy proposed, and three months later they were married.

"It was a whirlwind of a romance, yet their deep devotion for one another and their covenant relationship with each other gave their families and friends peace of mind and heart. There was no doubt in anyone's minds that the Father was in complete control of their relationship. Conroy also honored I-Jun's father by asking for his blessing to marry his daughter. He respected him in his role of father, and this allowed her family to see his character through the lens of the Father.

"Let's witness this next moment of their lives."

I was in awe of what I had just heard, and I deeply looked forward to seeing more of the next part of their marriage. I watched as the loving couple made their way into my secret beach.

"I-Jun, I'm so glad we were able to take a sabbatical and enjoy a week for our four year anniversary." Conroy gazed at his wife, admiring her beauty.

"Me too. It's so nice my parents agreed to watch the kids so we could be here."

I watched as they took out their towels and sat down by the waters, studying the marvelous view the Father had created.

"Conroy, I am so very blessed to have you as my husband. I praise and thank the Father daily for giving me you."

"I feel the same way."

"I was talking with my sister and she was sharing with me how she and my brother-in-law have been struggling to keep the passion alive. I realized that we haven't had that problem. What makes our relationship different, 여보(yeo bo)?"

Conroy thought a bit before responding. 'Holy Spirit, please give me the right words to express what You have revealed to me,' he prayed silently.

"Honey, I have actually been thinking about this for awhile now. When the Father started getting me ready for relationship, one thing I heard from people over and over is how once you are married, the feelings and attraction will fade, and that the relationship keeps going out of covenant relationship, and that's what will carry us through.

"I really struggled with that. I began to wonder how these feelings, this attraction, would go away, and how it would be possible for the relationship to grow just based out of action."

"I remember my married friends talking about that as well, 여보(yeo bo). They would say, 'eventually the feelings go away, the passion wanes, but although the feelings change the marriage goes on because then it's a choice to love. I think there is truth in that, but I also feel like something isn't quite right about it. I just can't put my finger on it." I-Jun looked out at the ocean as she tried to process her thoughts.

Conroy nodded. "Well, let me share with you some insight the Father gave me. I believe that covenant marriages continue on when faced with challenges, obstacles, and hardship (including passion waning) because we choose to love and put action to our words regardless of what we are feeling. As we talked about before, our feelings and emotions can lie to us, and if we make decisions based on them we can fall flat on our face. Therefore, when we choose to walk in love in our marriages, we will also choose to stay faithful and walk in spirit.

"Yet something that the Holy Spirit has been showing me goes back to Revelations 2:4 (NIV) which says, '4 Yet I hold this against you: You have forsaken the love you had at first.' I began to ponder this verse in my heart. Yeshua was telling the church of Ephesus that they had done right in discerning spirits and false prophets and teachers, but they had forgotten Him as their first love. They had lost their passion for Him, they had stopped pursuing Him as a lover.

"As I was pondering this, Revelations 2:5 (NIV) stood out to me. It says, '5 Consider how far you have fallen! Repent and do the things you did at first. If you do not repent, I will come to you and remove your lampstand from its place.' And I was blown away. Yeshua was telling them to rekindle the passion and fire again. And in order for them to do that, they first needed to repent of losing it, and then choose to do what they did at the very beginning of their relationship with Him.

"Then I started thinking, if Yeshua was telling the church to bring back the fire, then this must apply to earthly relationships too.”

“That makes sense. If we lose our fire, love, and passion for Yeshua and become lukewarm, then Yeshua tells us to turn up the flame and choose to get it back, or grow cold. In Revelations 3:16 (NIV) says, ’ [16] So, because you are lukewarm—neither hot nor cold—I am about to spit you out of my mouth.’ It’s very obvious that Yeshua is telling them to become hot again. So has He said anything about how this applies to relationships here on earth?” I-Jun looked intently at her husband, waiting for his response.

“Actually, yes He has. He brought me to Proverbs 5:15-20 (NIV) which says, ’ [15] Drink water from your own cistern, running water from your own well. [16] Should your springs overflow in the streets, your streams of water in the public squares? [17] Let them be yours alone, never to be shared with strangers. [18] May your fountain be blessed, and may you rejoice in the wife of your youth. [19] A loving doe, a graceful deer— may her breasts satisfy you always, may you ever be intoxicated with her love. [20] Why, my son, be intoxicated with another man’s wife? Why embrace the bosom of a wayward woman?’ Basically what the Holy Spirit is saying is that a husband should only drink from that of his wife, that the husband’s seed should not be shared with other women, forever affecting their offspring, but should only be given to his wife to affect their own offspring. The Holy Spirit is saying that the wife’s body should bring delight, intoxication, and fulfillment to a husband.

“I love how it references, ‘the wife of your youth’ because it shows that a man can easily forget his first love. Yet, the Father makes it clear that isn’t supposed to be the case. The love a husband has for his wife and her body should be passionate. And she should be sought after.”

“Hmmm…you know, 여보(yeo bo), I’ve heard so many Christians talking about sex and desire for a spouse, and it seems to me that passion is not something they agree with.”

"You caught that too?"

I-Jun nodded. "What has the Holy Spirit shown you about that?"

"I have heard so many men say they don't want to lust after their wives and her body. I had to pause and take that to the Father. What He showed me is that these husbands wanted their wife's body, wanted sex, but they had no desire to truly love her (her heart). Therefore, they would downplay the passion.

"I think the church has done a horrible job describing the difference between lust and passion in marriage. Because if passion, sex, and wanting your wife's body are wrong, then Song of Songs shouldn't be in the Bible."

I-Jun laughed. "I didn't even think about that. But you're right. It is very obvious throughout the whole of Song of Songs that the husband and wife are physically attracted to each other and desiring of one another. Their passion is on full display for all to see. So what do you think are the most important reasons for how our passion has been kept alive?"

"It's because at the very beginning of our relationship, darling, I pursued you. It wasn't about winning your heart, it wasn't about 'conquering' you in order for us to get married. I pursued your heart to know you and be known by you. Because I am pursuing your heart, that never stops or changes, even in marriage. I continue to pursue you, I plan out romantic dates, I figure out ways that I can honor and bless you, and I actively pursue your heart and your thoughts. I take time for you, and I keep my physical body in top shape to keep your eyes on me alone. Not only that, but I actively cultivate the right heart and spirit. Who I am on the inside needs to attract you as well. Everything I do is to keep our love hot and passionate.

"Even though we have five kids, I refuse to let this fire go out. Although we have moments where we have to choose spirit over flesh, love over selfishness, we have not lost our first love. We fight to keep our relationship strong, pure, and passionate.

Among our friends who are struggling with passion, how many husbands have stopped pursuing their wives' hearts, and how many wives have become distracted as mothers?"

I-Jun nodded in understanding of this truth. "여보 (yeo bo), let's find something to eat and keep talking. I am getting hungry."

Conroy laughed and stood, then helped his beloved wife to her feet.

I watched them walk away, beginning to understand how this very topic had affected my own marriage. Now that I was single again, I was starting to see what was really missing.

Chapter 36

"Aubrey, I have laid out a towel for you. Come, sit and talk with Me."

My eyes followed His nudging and I saw the towel laid out in a shaded area with a beautiful view of the ocean. I made my way over there, getting myself situated, longing to talk with the Holy Spirit about all that I had witnessed.

"Aubrey, what stood out to you from what you witnessed?"

"It was amazing reconnecting with some couples from previous witnesses, and I loved seeing their growth and how they were learning to be as one. Anastasia and Ethan showed me the importance of communication and hearing both sides. So many times in marriages you hear the spouse saying, 'my husband/wife should put my needs and wants first if he/she really cares about me.' And yet they fail to do the same for their spouse. The Father showed me that He wants those in covenant relationships to put the other person's needs first, and work together so the needs and wants of both are met.

"I also recognized the importance of honor and respect. The Father wants us to honor one another because, first of all, we are the Father's children, and second, the Father created each one of us and so we have value and worth. Honor should be given no matter how the other person responds or treats you. Respect, however, is an earned response. It's given after that individual has proven themself to be faithful, gentle, honest, etc.

"I saw the importance of correcting one another in love. The verses they shared from Ephesians 5:21-28 really impacted me. The new wineskin that the Father has for His children is so simple. None of this is actually new. It's all in the Bible, it's just that many in the old church have failed to obey (they don't know how to apply it) or even search out these treasures.

"I loved how they talked about filling each other up instead of draining one another of energy, hope, and love. Yet, there are too many times I have seen married couples draining their spouse and never giving back to fill them up. It all becomes so one-sided."

"Excellent points, Aubrey. Communication is a skill that many lack. People have become so easily offended and don't believe they should be corrected. They even silence My voice and eventually grow numb to My conviction. Humility and a willingness to learn and grow from one another is so important. There is no place for pride in the marriages the Father wants."

"That is a good point, Holy Spirit. I have witnessed many husbands full of pride who won't even receive a wife's wisdom and counsel, and treat her as a trophy to be silenced and owned. However, there are also just as many women who are so prideful that they refuse to let their spouse speak into their lives. Pride really has no place in a relationship.

"Jeremiah and Emily were so adorable. I loved seeing their growth. I could relate so very much to Emily and her past. I experienced gaslighting and the silent treatment, and I have often wondered if, should my future spouse respond the same way, would I be triggered, or would I see him for the godly man he is?

"Our pasts can play such a huge role in our futures if we don't take care of the baggage. In order to have a better future we need to forgive those who hurt us, or even forgive ourselves. We need to heal from broken dreams, traumas and hurts, and brokenness. We need to break off all lies that we have believed that are contrary to the Father's thoughts on us, and we need to put habits in place that will allow us to respond in spirit and not in flesh.

"Too many individuals jump into marriage or a relationship before they're ready. They bring their old responses, old belief systems, and old habits into the new relationship and are so hopeful for a different outcome. Yet they do not let go of the past and heal. I loved how they both understood that although it wasn't intentional, the trauma connected each one's response to the past. They both worked together to understand one another's hearts and made things right quickly.

"Jeremiah let go of his anger and chose gentleness. He acted out Colossians 3:19 (NIV) which says, '19 Husbands, love your wives and do not be harsh with them.' Emily chose to see Jeremiah through the Father's eyes. It was really beautiful to witness and gave me hope for my future. Because I know that the Father will bring me a husband who will challenge me, but also walk with me through the challenges. I also loved how they chose to communicate openly instead of hiding what was bothering them. Again, communicating and choosing to hear the other person without putting your own spin on what they are saying is so very important."

"Well done, Aubrey. You see how the heart and mind are truly where battles are fought and won. When you allow your thoughts and views of others to override what is actually true and how the Father sees them, you begin to lose the battle in communication and relationship. But when you keep the Father's perspective about them at the forefront, victories are won and satan loses his power."

"It's true though, isn't it, Holy Spirit? So many of our

battles in marriage and things we believe are struggles, really boil down to putting ourselves first before the other. It's putting our thoughts before the Father's and trusting in our own judgements when we don't even have a clear picture or understanding of the truth. All these situations we witnessed appeared easy to navigate, but truthfully, when we are in the moment, the situation always feels extreme. But really, it's simple too. It's when we become busy and tired, we want our needs met, we are focused on being heard but unwilling to listen, and even when our flesh rises up that it actually becomes very difficult to walk in spirit and in love.

"I loved seeing Adelyn and Do-Yun's relationship. I loved seeing how they balanced family, ministry, and marriage. They were the Ephesians 5:31 (NIV) couple which says, '31 "For this reason a man will leave his father and mother and be united to his wife, and the two will become one flesh."' They worked together for the Kingdom of God, and because they had the right balance, not one area suffered. I feel like that's really difficult for most in leadership. They either put their spouses first, ministries first, or children first, and eventually all suffer. But Adelyn and Do-Yun put the Father first and gave You full authority to work in and through their lives. They found a balance, and their anointing and purpose thrived.

"I absolutely loved meeting the new couple, I-Jun and Conroy. They were another couple that understood how to do marriage, family, and ministry together. So many times you see it tiered as the Father at the top, then spouse, then kids, and finally, ministry. But I-Jun and Conroy had the Father, Yeshua, and You at the center and then their marriage, kids, and ministry circled around the Trinity. They allowed You to lead them, and that meant that all three were important and none suffered. There was give and take, there was working together to meet any needs and to be there for one another, and all of it brought glory to the Father.

"Holy Spirit, that is the type of marriage I want. I want to learn how to have a 'sphere' marriage, family, and ministry, that circles and intertwines with one another because the Trinity is at the center of it all."

"I am glad that you want that marriage, because that is exactly the marriage the Father has for you. He understands that His children don't have the time like they used too, and He also redeems time. You were forced, and at times chose, to give up ministry, family, etc. because of your spouse. The Father is going to redeem those years and you will find that all three (marriage, family, and ministry) will be intertwined, circling within each other, with the Trinity as the core. In order to navigate a new blueprint, it will be important to listen to Me and follow My leading. You will make mistakes as you learn, but I will correct you in love and bring you back into alignment. Don't give up, and always keep the Father at the center."

"Holy Spirit, I really loved how Conroy was convicted about his anger and immediately made it right with his children. He showed them the importance of obedience to the Father through both word and action. In turn, his children were able to follow his example and position their hearts before the Father too, making things right. And I loved seeing I-Jun loving on her children. She was active in their lives. Even though she was tired, she wasn't lazy or 'there' but not there. She was present, and she met their physical and emotional needs. Her children knew she loved them, and they were healthy and content in that.

"I love how the parents showed what going above and beyond looks like towards one another, and how their children were able to apply what they were witnessing to each other and their parents too. It shows the power of parents who love one another and walk in spirit. The impact they have on their children is so very strong. No wonder in Luke 17:2 (NIV) says, '2 It would be better for them to be thrown into the sea with a millstone tied around their neck than to cause one of these little ones to stumble.' If a parent becomes a stumbling block to their child's relationship with the Father, then He will bring judgment and correction towards the parent. For they did not steward their gifts (children) in a way that honored the Father."

"That is an excellent point, Aubrey. Many children will go on to have unhealthy marriages because they follow the example set by their parents. Husband and wives need to walk in the new blueprint, allowing full access to the Trinity, because they affect their children's futures and how they see the Trinity. Colossians 3:21 (NIV) says, '21 Fathers, do not embitter your children, or they will become discouraged.'"

"Holy Spirit, I have to admit, the last thing we witnessed about I-Jun and Conroy really hit home. My ex-husband actually said that he chose not to have sex at times, because he didn't want to lust after me. Other times he would withhold it for long times in-between because he was using it as a weapon, a means to hurt me. I really struggled to understand how lust could even be a part in a marriage. I read Song of Songs as a young teenager and it was very evident they were on fire, passionate about sex and each other's bodies.

"It made so much sense when Conroy shared how passion turns to lust when a spouse is longing for the feeling of sex, but isn't willing to love their spouse in spirit. Lust is about selfishness and meeting your own needs, whereas passion and desire are about experiencing something together because you love one another and want the other one to feel and know your love and passion for them.

"I have heard countless times that many believers and churches remove sex from the conversation table. It reminds me of when I was going to school for Interior Design and had an art class. I had to write an essay about sex in art, and I talked about the believer and Song of Songs. I remember one classmate asking me if believers really believed that about sex, because everything they had heard about Christians and from churches was that the point of sex is to create a baby and isn't to be enjoyed or experienced unless children are the goal.

"I was really surprised to hear afterwards that many Christians believe this way. But that is not what the Father intended for sex and intimacy in marriage. The Father's children should have passionate, fiery marriages that make the world wish they could have the same. Believers should be leading the way in what a holy, pure, passionate sexual desire is all about.

"I found the revelation concerning what Yeshua tells the church about getting away from being lukewarm and rekindling their first love for Him, so very important. If we are to live that way for Him, then the excuses spouses give for no longer having passion in their marriage also goes back to that they have forgotten their first love for their spouse. In a lot of ways this is found in busyness, selfishness, tiredness, walking in flesh, etc., all of which affect the passion we have for our spouse. We stop taking care of our outward appearances, and we stop taking time to pursue one another."

"It's true, Aubrey. How many married couples have you seen who are strangers in the same house?"

"Too many to count. I like how the couples we witnessed understood the difference between winning the heart and pursuing the heart. Once they got married, they still pursued each other. Winning to own was never the intention. Instead it was the lifelong desire to pursue until eternity. Holy Spirit, that means going on dates was still important, writing letters (songs, pictures, etc.) of love, communicating at all times with purposefulness and listening to each other without being distracted, and continuing to make time for one another. They didn't let business, distractions, or life take them away from the pursuit of one another.

"But honestly, Holy Spirit, isn't that the way most believers become lukewarm, because they fail to pursue the Father?"

"You are right. Believers stop spending quality time with the Father and eventually as they spend less and less time in His presence, the fire of their first love begins to die out."

"Which is why choosing to love and to be in spirit is also important. Because we need to choose to prioritize our spouses. We need to choose to protect our families."

"Exactly, Aubrey. Do you remember when I brought you to the mountain top when we were discussing dating and engagement?"

"I remember."

"At that time, you talked about the view you saw, but do you remember anything from the actual top of the mountain you stood on?"

"Hmmm...I remember that I was surprised because I thought the top of the mountain would have more of a tip to it, but once we got to it, there was about thirty feet of flat ground."

"There is a reason the Father wanted that mountain to be flat on top rather than come to a point. Many believers and leaders talk about singles standing on each side of a pyramid, and as they move up the pyramid they will at times connect with their future spouse and then bounce away. But at the top is the Father, and as they draw close to the Father, they in turn draw close to one another. Finally, they connect at the point and begin their married life with God at center. Then comes the tiered layer of the old way of marriage.

"But the Father wants you to know that as you draw close to Him, you are carrying Me with you. You are not striving to finally reach the Father, because you have already reached Him. So as you are moving your way up the pyramid, you are actually actively waiting, or taking active courage by being obedient to what the Father calls you to do until you are joined with your spouse. Your future spouse is doing the same, and as each of you step through open doors, you finally come to a place where you are both standing at the end of two doors facing each other. As the doorbells ring and you open them wide, there you both stand with a hallway connecting you.

"Now visualize the top of the mountain. The doors open and you find yourself at the top, facing each other, with thirty feet of flat ground in-between you. Now isn't the time to walk to each other, **NO**, now it's time to run towards each other. This is when the Father will accelerate and merge you together. You will know him, and he will know you. You will have such a deep connection and understanding of each other, and as you run towards one another, all other things the Father has you doing will accelerate too, until you collide and your lives become one. Your ministries and callings will begin to circle each other, and you will find that all along the Father led you to run towards each other and you were never the only one running."

"I needed that, Holy Spirit. So many times I feel like I am alone in the waiting for him and making my way to him, but You are right, he is also running towards me."

"Aubrey, Song of Songs 8:6-7 (NIV) says, '6 Place me like a seal over your heart, like a seal on your arm; for love is as strong as death, its jealousy unyielding as the grave. It burns like blazing fire, like a mighty flame. 7 Many waters cannot quench love; rivers cannot sweep it away. If one were to give all the wealth of one's house for love, it would be utterly scorned.'

"Aubrey, I know that you noticed your hair changing color during each phase of relationship. Is there anything you would like to ask Me concerning it?"

"Actually, yes, Holy Spirit. Why was my hair changing colors? Is there a detail from the Father in it?"

"Yes, there are details from the Father. During the first phase of relationship, brother and sister, your hair was purple. Purple is symbolic of royalty. The Father wants His children to remember that each of you are royalty. You belong to His family, and therefore, all of your actions, responses, and words should reflect who you belong to. Phase two of relationship was that of boyfriend/girlfriend and engaged. There, your hair was blue. Blue represents wisdom. However, the Father doesn't mean just any wisdom, but wisdom that comes from Him. He is calling His children to be wise and discerning, to know the seasons and times you are living in, and to follow My leading. Phase three of relationship was marriage and families, and your hair was blonde. Blonde represents the Father's call to be His pure Bride. It's a call to purity and to the revealing of the ancient key. This ancient key has been hidden for a long time, but now the Father has given it to you to run with and unlock the doors of relationships."

Chapter 37

"Aubrey, now I want you to take some time and share the blueprints to this ancient key, that I have put in your heart. It's time to write the vision and run."

"Yes, Holy Spirit."

Blueprints for Relationship

In order to have healthy relationships, we need to go back to the very basic foundation. That foundation is our relationship with the Father, with Yeshua, and with the Holy Spirit. In Beyond Held Hostage, I laid out the framework for restoring and rekindling our relationship with the Trinity. Throughout our journey, the Holy Spirit has relentlessly made our need to have Him in our daily lives, very obvious.

The first important thing is to accept Jesus as Lord and Savior of your life. To realize that you are a sinner saved by grace through Jesus, who died on the cross for you, defeated satan and the grave, rose again, went to heaven, and one day soon will return for us. Nothing we do will make us clean and perfect, we were born in sin and we die in sin, unless we repent and believe in Jesus. He is the only way to heaven, to the Father. John 3:16 (NIV) says, "[16] For God so loved the world that he gave his one and only Son, that whoever believes in him shall not perish but have eternal life."

Many of us have a very flawed view of the Father. We see Him as a judgmental being in the sky who is just waiting for us to make a mistake and set us up for judgement. I have seen fathers who set up their children for failure (sin) and how they got a sense of pleasure from correcting their child. Yet, that is not the Father. He does not set us up to fall into sin. No, He corrects and disciplines in love, and the goal is always reconciliation with Him. 1 John 3:1 (NIV) says, "[1] See what great love the Father has lavished on us, that we should be called children of God! And that is what we are! The reason the world does not know us is that it did not know him."

We need to understand the role of the Father, the Son Yeshua, and the Holy Spirit. The Word (Bible) clearly reveals what each of their roles are, how they work together and are one, and the relationship they want with us. John 14:15-17 (NIV) says, "[15] "If you love me, keep my commands. [16] And I will ask the Father, and he will give you another advocate to help you and be with you forever— [17] the Spirit of truth. The world cannot accept him, because it neither sees him nor knows him. But you know him, for he lives with you and will be in you."

We need to understand what Biblical, covenant relationship is with the Trinity, and how that applies to our relationship with Them. "A covenant is a binding contract that will not become void or left unfulfilled."[7] Once we understand this kind of relationship, then we are to apply it to our relationship with our spouse. "The Father is all about true covenant relationship. Now remember the Father, the Son, and the Holy Spirit are good. There is no evil in Them, They do not lie, deceive, or break Their promises. They fulfill and remain faithful even when we do not."[8]

We need to learn how to hear the voice of the Father, and how to listen to the Holy Spirit. John 10:16 (NIV) says, "[16] I have other sheep that are not of this sheep pen. I must bring them also. They too will listen to my voice, and there shall be one flock and one shepherd." Also Isaiah 30:21 (NIV) says, "[21] Whether you turn to the right or to the left, your ears will hear a voice behind you, saying, "This is the way; walk in it." The Holy Spirit wants us to use the gifts of the Spirit that He imparts to us in order to bring the Kingdom of God to the world, and encourage the new church. 1 Corinthians 12:8-11 (NIV) says, "[8] To one there is

---

[7] Aubrey Dawn Weinzetl, "Beyond Held Hostage." 2023.

[8] Aubrey Dawn Weinzetl, "Beyond Held Hostage." 2023

given through the Spirit a message of wisdom, to another a message of knowledge by means of the same Spirit, [9] to another faith by the same Spirit, to another gifts of healing by that one Spirit, [10] to another miraculous powers, to another prophecy, to another distinguishing between spirits, to another speaking in different kinds of tongues, and to still another the interpretation of tongues. [11] All these are the work of one and the same Spirit, and he distributes them to each one, just as he determines."

We need to understand our Tribe and the people the Father has placed in our lives, as well as our role for ministry. Ephesians 4:11-13 (NIV) says, "[11] So Christ himself gave the apostles, the prophets, the evangelists, the pastors and teachers, [12] to equip his people for works of service, so that the body of Christ may be built up [13] until we all reach unity in the faith and in the knowledge of the Son of God and become mature, attaining to the whole measure of the fullness of Christ." In Acts 2, we find that the Tribe (Bride) were together in unity. They provided for and took care of one another (not relying on government); every day they gathered and worshipped, ate together, and their tongues were filled with thanksgiving. The Father daily brought more and more people into the Kingdom. The Tribe was there for one another, and within their unity the gifts of the Spirit would manifest and strengthen the Kingdom of God. We need to be brave and courageous though, for the times we live in would weaken us and keep us from being involved in the ministries the Father calls us to. Joshua 1:9 (NIV) says, "[9] Have I not commanded you? Be strong and courageous. Do not be afraid; do not be discouraged, for the LORD your God will be with you wherever you go."

We need to know how to use our spiritual weapons to defeat the enemy. We need to walk in spirit, not in flesh, guarding our thoughts and keeping them holy and aligned with the Father, and cultivating a heart of thanksgiving. Hebrews 10:22-25 (NIV) says, "[22] let us draw near to God with a sincere heart and with the full assurance that faith brings, having our hearts sprinkled to cleanse us from a guilty conscience and having our bodies washed with pure water. [23] Let us hold unswervingly to the hope we profess, for he who promised is faithful. [24] And let us consider how we may spur one another on toward love and good deeds, [25] not giving up meeting together, as some are in the habit of doing, but encouraging one another—and all the more as you see the Day approaching."

We need to be healthy in spirit, mind, and physical body, for each of these areas can affect our relationship with the Father.

We need to fight and not allow satan to take any ground. Instead, we charge forward, taking ground for the Father and closing the doors we opened to satan. 1 Peter 5:8-9 (NIV) says, "[8] Be alert and of sober mind. Your enemy the devil prowls around like a roaring lion looking for someone to devour. [9] Resist him, standing firm in the faith, because you know that the family of believers throughout the world is undergoing the same kind of sufferings." Also Ephesians 6:11-13 (NIV) says, "[11] Put on the full armor of God, so that you can take your stand against the devil's schemes. [12] For our struggle is not against flesh and blood, but against the rulers, against the authorities, against the powers of this dark world and against the spiritual forces of evil in the heavenly realms. [13] Therefore put on the full armor of God, so that when the day of evil comes, you may be able to stand your ground, and after you have done everything, to stand." While we are warring spiritually, we are also reclaiming ourselves, our ministries, our callings, habits, hobbies, and relationships, and using them for the glory of the Father.

In Beyond Held Hostage there are a couple of sentences that seem very fitting to use here:

"I pray that the last sixteen weeks has propelled you forward into new beginnings with God. Everything that you have learned, and what God has taken you through is meant to be applied for the rest of your life. These are not just steps for breakthrough, but they are a lifestyle of relationship with God."[9]

If we are not living out our relationship with the Trinity every day, then we will not be able to carry the new blueprints for relationship. Why? Because every blueprint stems from our relationship with the Trinity. When we walk in spirit instead of flesh, we are living examples of the Father. When we let the Holy Spirit move in our days freely, we are led through open doors and opportunities to be used for the Father. If we are not in relationship with the Father, we will not be able to stand against satan. Eventually we will find ourselves dying and satan winning in our lives.

We need to break every sin that holds us hostage. We need freedom from every habit that leads us away from the Father. We need to heal from every wound and trauma, and remove every root that is infested with wickedness from our hearts. We need to let go of all baggage from our pasts so we don't carry it into our future relationships, both earthly and with the Trinity.

So the very first thing to do is rekindle your relationship with the Trinity. Begin to live your life in obedience with the Word (Bible), and most importantly, give the Trinity room to work in your life and interrupt your days. Once you are in alignment and no longer living of the world, you are ready to carry the blueprints for relationships. 2 Corinthians 3:17-18 (NIV) says, "[17] Now the Lord is the Spirit, and where the Spirit of the Lord is, there is freedom. [18] And we all, who with unveiled faces contemplate the Lord's glory, are being transformed into his image with ever-increasing glory, which comes from the Lord, who is the Spirit."

---

[9] Aubrey Dawn Weinzetl, "Beyond Held Hostage". 2023.

Brother and Sister Relationship

In relationships we need to be wise and discerning, not looking at it from the world's view, but through the Father's eyes. When we are communicating in Brother and Sister relationships, we need to be wise with the words and tones we use. We should be encouraging one another in reaching our full potential and callings. It is important to correct one another in love, not letting anyone be led astray, but directing them back to the Father.

The Father has created us to belong to a Tribe, to have a group of people that we can connect with and spur on in each's race.

It is very important that the Holy Spirit leads us in these relationships, because emotions and feelings and our own perspectives can easily be used by satan to destroy and tear down the relationship. We should never be a weapon that satan uses.

In Brother and Sister relationships we should include the Holy Spirit and allow Him to be with us, and we should be seeking the Father together. That means worshiping the Father together, speaking in tongues together, letting the gifts of the spirit be manifested and used. As we bring the Trinity into our conversations and activities, it removes any room that satan would want to steal. The door is firmly shut in his face.

It is important that we view brothers/sisters as brothers and sisters in Christ, recognizing that they were created in the image of the Father and are His sons and daughters. That means we should hold each other in honor and esteem. No evil should come out of our mouths. We should guard one another, protect one another, correct one another, and build one another up. James 5:19-20 (NIV) says, "[19] My brothers and sisters, if one of you should wander from the truth and someone should bring that person back, [20] remember this: Whoever turns a sinner from the error of their way will save them from death and cover over a multitude of sins."

We need to be wise in how the world sees us, so we do not become a stumbling block to them joining the family of God.

That means we are wise in one-on-one activities. We are aware of the time of day that we get together, and are careful not to give room for reputations to be stained with gossip and malice. We protect sensitive information, and we don't throw pearls to swine. Not every detail should be shared with a brother and sister, and we should allow the Holy Spirit to give us the right wording, as well, if we should share, or if we are to wait.

I think it is important to acknowledge that most of our problems come into being because we are putting ourselves first before others. Even this week, I was thinking about how when someone says something to me and I take it personally, I realize that I need to step back and actually find out the heart behind what was said. We forget that each one of us is going through this world and we face many similar problems, hurts, and concerns. We respond harshly without thinking of how that hurts another. We need to understand that our words hold power, and we can destroy another person or lift them up. But we also need to give grace to other individuals and understand their heart as well. The Father calls us to forgive and give second chances. Matthew 18:21-22 (NIV) says, "[21] Then Peter came to Jesus and asked, "Lord, how many times shall I forgive my brother or sister who sins against me? Up to seven times?" [22] Jesus answered, "I tell you, not seven times, but seventy-seven times."

Grace, compassion, and love, used with correction, reveals how we can build one another up. Everything contrary to the Father and the Word must be removed from our thoughts, hearts, and the foundation of our beliefs. Through love, we are able to build the foundation and walls back up, realigning us with the Father's design.

So many times when we are hurt, we respond in that hurt, which leads us to sin. Instead we need to respond in Spirit. Jesus is our greatest example of love and correction. We need to follow His example, and that means listening to the Holy Spirit.

Now when it comes to second chances, we are not talking about those who are abusive and being used as demonic weapons for the enemy, but those who are following the Father and are still learning. We are to forgive even those who do not belong to the Father, but we do not give them authority to move in our lives or speak into our futures. We listen to the Holy Spirit, and we choose wise counsel. However, we show love and honor to all.

One of the biggest things I have noticed is that believers are becoming less open and vulnerable. We tend to hide our faults and mistakes, and even sins that we still commit. We find ourselves held hostage, instead of living in freedom. When we are not open and vulnerable, we choose not to let the Father use us to help others from making the same mistakes and sins we have. What would happen if the church became open? What would happen if we were honest about our feelings, emotions, and hearts? What would happen if we responded in love instead of judgment and were used by the Father to bring healing to that individual? What would happen to relationships that are built in the honesty and freedom to speak from the heart?

We should protect one another's hearts. We should learn to understand the heart behind each person, and we should learn how to communicate without judgement, offense, and selfishness.

We should actively work to represent the Trinity in a way that is holy.

"[23] "I have the right to do anything," you say—but not everything is beneficial. "I have the right to do anything"—but not everything is constructive. [24] No one should seek their own good, but the good of others." 1 Corinthians 10:23-24 (NIV)

Dating and Engagement Relationships

Again, the Holy Spirit needs to be a part of these relationships. We need to be wise and aware of how satan wants to destroy the blueprints for the new relationships. We need to be led forth in peace, and we need to be positioned at all times to respond to the Holy Spirit.

We need to live in complete honesty and truth. When we are dating and engaged, we should not change ourselves just to be accepted and then return to who we really are. That is being fake, and there is nothing honoring in that. In actuality, it's manipulative and destructive for relationships.

We should live lives that are open and full of vulnerability, willing to be responsible for our pasts. Our testimonies are an important part of what the Father has done in our lives and we should let our future spouse into this intimate area. We should be honest about our family situations and how that will affect a future together. Face it, when you get married, you are also marrying into each other's families and cultures. Therefore, we should be honest about our families, friends, and our pasts. This allows relationships to become stronger, and satan can't use them later as a tool to destroy the relationship. Honesty, trust, and faithfulness are key characteristics for relationships.

When individuals are dating, they should not be communicating one-on-one-with other friends of the opposite sex or doing one-on-one activities. This is not honoring to their significant other, and does not show their value and worth. When one enters into a dating or engaged relationship then they need to change. Not change their heart and character, but change the way they respond to situations and individuals. When one continues to act like they are single, they fail to be faithful. Obedience to the Father is important, and if we fail to obey the Word our relationships will struggle. A lot of people also talk about having boundaries with others. My position on this is that if we are following the leading of the Holy Spirit daily, He will keep us on the path of righteousness. When we are kept on the path of righteousness, there is no room for sin and wickedness. Therefore, our boundary is the Holy Spirit.

The relationship should not be focused on winning a person, but on pursuing their heart. We should be asking the Holy Spirit if the person we are interested in is the one we should pursue. The Father knows the heart of each individual, He knows if the person is seeking Him or not. How many individuals jump into relationship without even asking the Holy Spirit for His leading? We make our own way happen and then blame the Father when it turns out to be a big mistake. No, ask first, and do not move on it until the Father has given a yes.

Make sure you position yourself in relationship with the Father. He is the one who leads His children together, matching them up. So be faithful, focus on bringing His Kingdom to the world. Be about His business, and watch as He writes a beautiful love story for you.

Again, communication is key. Be willing to be corrected in love, respond in humility, be gentle, caring, considerate, and make lasting memories that overshadow satan's attacks, and learn to meet your significant other's needs. Our actions should always align with the Word (Bible), and as we allow the Holy Spirit to lead us, we will find freedom in communication.

Sex before marriage is a NO! It is sin and it is wrong. Do not live with one another before marriage, for it is sin as well, and a door to temptation that satan will take full advantage of.

Stay faithful to one another, always moving with the Holy Spirit. Spend time as a couple in the presence of the Father. Do Bible studies together, worship together, pray together, prophecy together, speak in tongues together, do ministry together, create hobbies that you both enjoy. Make room for each other in your daily lives. Go out of your way to let each other know how much you love and appreciate the other.

A great example of this is, one of the witnesses the Holy Spirit expanded on this week. It was when He revealed to me that Ethan knew he would marry Anastasia, but he didn't have the proposal planned out. He was following the leading of the Holy Spirit, even in the proposal. The Holy Spirit led him to a beautiful lake-side proposal that may have appeared random and sporadic, but was a detail the Father had planned.

Married and Family Relationships

Each one of us has different callings, gifts, talents, and ministries, and there is going to be no 'one-blueprint-fits-all.' We are all created to be unique and so it will be very important to listen to the Father and follow the leading of the Holy Spirit.

Husbands and wives have great power to destroy one another. If we leave our tongues and tones unguarded, and allow evil thoughts to take root in our hearts about each other, we will be used by satan to destroy one another. Husbands and wives can become the greatest tool to prevent each other from following the Father and reaching their full potential. Husbands and wives are meant to support one another, carry each other's burdens, and meet each other's needs. Ecclesiastes 4:9-12 (NIV) says, "[9] Two are better than one, because they have a good return for their labor: [10] If either of them falls down, one can help the other up. But pity anyone who falls and has no one to help them up. [11] Also, if two lie down together, they will keep warm. But how can one keep warm alone? [12] Though one may be overpowered, two can defend themselves. A cord of three strands is not quickly broken."

We must protect one another. We must walk out the fruit of the spirit towards one another. It's not optional! We need to be obedient to the Word (Bible) in order to have healthy relationships. We should meet each other's needs, filling each other up, encouraging one another on, and speaking life over each other. We should not nag or be negative, but ask for the Father's perspective at all times. When we allow our jokes, our teasing, and our words to become harmful to our spouse and kids, we have brought judgment on ourselves. We will be held accountable either here on earth or in heaven. All of our actions have consequences. If we are making good choices, then there will be good consequences, but when we fail and sin there will be negative consequences. There is no excuse for affairs.

Pride and anger have no place in a marriage or family. These need to be corrected immediately, with habits put in place so one does not destroy that which the Father has set them over. It is important to learn how to do spiritual warfare together, not fight against one another. For we do not wage war against one another, but against the enemy.

We need to keep the Trinity, our spouses, and our family as top priority. We should not let life get busy and stop investing in these relationships. Take time to cultivate the marriage and continue to pursue one another. Learn how to balance it all. Do not let your spouse, your kids, or your ministry suffer. Learn how the Father wants you to respond with each, and how He is going to direct your sphere.

Keep the fire in your marriage going. Write love letters (take notes from Song of Songs), create romantic dinners and dates that keep that passion and love alive, and work hard to keep your outward appearance healthy and appealing to your spouse so their eyes are on you alone. Too many times women let themselves go when they have kids because they are tired and drained. Make an effort to present the very best outward you that compliments the inward you. Men should make sure they also keep physically fit and appearance sharp.

When times get hard, when flesh rises up, choose to walk in spirit and to love. No matter what, don't let satan win. When mistakes are made, things are spoken, immediately correct it and bring reconciliation. Don't allow satan any room to use words and mistakes to destroy what the Father has brought together.

We should be making life fun and enjoyable, with memories that we will be able to leave our children and grandchildren with. What areas in life do you find difficult, boring, or irritating? Ask the Holy Spirit how a husband and wife and family can make these enjoyable, honoring experiences and responsibilities.

It is important that we learn how to compromise for one

another, that we are making sure each of our needs are being met. We should not come across as nagging, but learn how to communicate, correct, and repent in a way that is honoring and glorifying to the Father. We also want to make sure that our communication is edifying for the family and ministry.

We need to understand that each of us has a past, and that we carry what we learned into our futures. Therefore, how we overcome our past responses, memories, and habits together is a key to victory in marriage. Again grace, love, and compassion will be needed to overcome trauma, mistakes, and old habits.

Learn how to do ministry together as a family, allowing the Holy Spirit to lead you to different opportunities. Pray together for direction and leading each day, and listen as a family for the Father's will for each day. If you find your family too busy, then work together to find out what areas need to be released so that the Father is given the time. When we do that, He has a way of blessing us back, and we don't regret what we give up here on earth.

Chapter 38

Here are some insights that can be applied to all three phases of relationship: to brother/sister, dating/engaged, and marriage and family. I have divided them up into categories.

One thing I want to mention is that the world has tried to strip men of their masculinity and make them feminine (they do this even to Jesus). This has never been the Father's heart for His sons. The world has also tried to change women, and it is important to realize that the Father created men to be men and women to be women. Many different movements have taken place through the years that have tried to tear away who the Father created us to be in the name of progress and equality.

If men are treating sisters-in-Christ as just that, then the sisters are protected, cherished, and provided for. They can also be a support for their brother-in-Christ and be someone they can rely on. If women are treating brothers-in-Christ as such, the brothers will be empowered to provide for the weak and needy, and be defenders of all. We should be showing the world how the Father intended men and women to be, how we take care of one another, encourage one another, stand with one another, and how each one of us is strong in the Father and full of unity.

Women are not weak and needy. We are full of courage and bravery. However, we should never strip men of who the Father made them to be and the authority He has given them, just to prove that we also have callings and gifts. Instead, women should support and battle alongside men in their role. Men in turn should give opportunities for women to support them shoulder to shoulder, and yet still protect them. We should learn how to rely on one another and encourage one another on in the 'faith.' If we are being obedient to the Word (Bible) and following the Holy Spirit, our young men will be men, and our young women will be women. We won't care about how the world sees us, and each one of us will be fulfilling the Father's plan for our lives and be who He created us to be.

These insights are for brother and sister relationship. However, they also apply to the other two categories of relationship, because they will continue on into those as well.
(The insights for dating and engaged will only carry over into marriage and family.)

*The Father is in charge of time. He will create magical moments in time that will close the distance and bring us closer to each other. He will also pause time when needed.

*Be aware of each other's families, friends, and be there to help them. (This will help carry the weight that the other carries).

*Learn how to have fun and accept godly teasing, and how to tease back.

*Give to one another, have each other's backs, observe each other's needs and how you meet them.

*Keep each other company and stay by each other's side in difficult or uncomfortable times and situations.

*Make sacrifices for each other.

*Be quick to forgive and don't hold grudges. Be brave and work at not misunderstanding. (Cultivate good communication.)

*Correct one another in love.

*Be open and honest, but there may be topics that are inappropriate to share, so be mindful.

*Have healthy individual habits in place. (How you communicate, how you exercise, eat, drink, what you wear, your morals and character, etc.)

*Recognize the other person's good qualities and encourage them in the things they do right. Don't always pick at the negative.

*Talk about uncomfortable topics bravely and come up with solutions together.

*Know when it's right to ask for help, and if it's appropriate, ask a family member or person of same sex.

*Gently call each other out regarding behaviors and habits that are bad or unhealthy.

*Correct and explain the consequences of what choices they are making. Bluntly tell it like it is, but then task the person with making the right decision out of their own free will. Don't let them run from the choice, though. Let them know you're aware of the wrong choices and then continue to encourage and challenge them to do it differently next time. Allow your relationship to change them. Through it all, apply love, care, gentleness, and kindness.

*There should be patience. Help to solve problems, but also don't be used or fooled. Honesty is always the best policy. Go down to the other person's level or learn how to help them rise up to your level.

*When someone gives vague answers, the other needs to trust, unless that individual has proven to be untrustworthy.

*When teasing, always let that person know it's just that, and make sure there are no misunderstandings. Don't let the teasing become harmful or hurtful.

*Be aware of each other's feelings, keep watch on if there needs to be changes to how things are shared and talk about it with one another.

*Make sure each person carries their responsibility, and support them even when it's hard.

*Don't fight against each other, but learn to understand each other's feelings and heart.

*Be considerate and aware of what the other likes and doesn't like, what they can or can't eat, etc.

*Give warnings and direction, but also listen and follow through.

*Have inside jokes and memories.

*Explain things in a way the other person will understand.

*Help one another even in embarrassing situations. Don't run from them. Do your best not to make the situation even more embarrassing.

*If you are easily embarrassed, don't let it control you, and realize that others are there to help you, not make you feel worse.

*Help keep one another at ease. When one is sick, help to take care of them.

*Although brother and sister, recognize that to honor means there is still a difference compared to a blood sibling.

*Men, walk the women home, make sure they arrive safely, and don't be overbearing in it. When walking in a group, make sure they are always close to the group and never alone. Defend each other, be vulnerable, give and receive comfort, and to **engaged and married couples**—carry her purse and bag.

*Be aware of the other's finances. (You don't need to see a bank account to know if they are struggling. Learn to observe what they buy, how they spend, and even what they say about finances.) If they are struggling, bless them and pay for them. Just make sure that they know you are only doing it as a brother or sister.

*Be vulnerable about your weaknesses, fears, and struggles. Knowing you accept each other and will continue to support one another will help create healthy individuals.

*Communicate with one another on how to respond to situations. Learn to do it in ways that are kind and not harsh; don't become prideful but remain humble. When rejecting others' help, always let them know you appreciate their heart.

*There will be times when fear comes in, but don't let it keep you from facing things. Encourage one another to confront those things head on. Keep trying even if you keep failing. Watch on with concern, respond and protect, and help heal each other's wounds in the Father.

*Don't be afraid to cry, and don't tell the other person to quit being a baby or grow up. Instead, comfort, and find ways to bring joy, laughter, and smiles.

*Talk about the person a brother/sister might want to date and give warnings if you recognize something isn't right in their dating life.

*Brothers and sisters should help each other mature and grow.

*Give one another good counsel and help them make right decisions. If that counsel lines up with the Word (Bible), then the individual should listen.

*Be brave and try new things even if you are not good at them. Don't embarrass each other when trying new things, but encourage. Make sure you don't let others bring embarrassment, or tease and hurt their feelings. Always have each other's back.

*Know which relationships to hold onto and which ones to let go of.

*Learn which jokes and teasing are appropriate for brother and sister, and which ones cross the line and should never be said, because they will harm the relationship, bring distrust, and open a door to satan to use.

Insights for dating and engaged relationships, that also carry into marriage and family relationships.

*Give good gifts.

*Although nervous about liking someone, don't hide from the feelings, and accept that you like that person. You don't need to be sneaky. Continue to be yourself, and you don't need to share right away that your feelings have changed to more. Be aware of the right time to share your feelings. Until then, silently love that person and care about them. Don't cause pressure, just continue to support, help, and let them know they can trust you with the deep stuff. (The Holy Spirit will lead you if you let Him.)

*Relationships should help each one grow in maturity, and each person should be the missing piece to their heart and help them fulfill the blueprints of their purpose and calling.

*Learn which jokes and teasing should take place after marriage.

*Listen to what the other person wants to do and do it without complaining. Each voice should be heard.

*Flirt and be bold in pursuing one another. Tease and flirt, make each other blush, but never be mean or inappropriate.

*Don't rush the process. Let your feelings be known, but also learn when to protect your feelings till the right time.

*Although a woman can pursue a man, there is something about a guy (even if he knows the girl likes him) still asking if he can pursue her with marriage in mind, where he is honest, direct, and doesn't play the dating game. He continues to pursue her until she is ready for a dating relationship.

*When you know that the other person likes you back, be brave and pursue. Overcome all fear.

*Don't change yourself, but remain true to who you are created to be. (This does not apply to sin and bad habits).

*Wait for the right time for kissing. Talk through what boundaries are good for you both, and don't force the physical side of relationship.

*Keep each other's secrets.

*Support one another's dreams and callings. When you know the other person is struggling with motivation, find ways to get them excited, and explain information in a way they will understand.

*Treasure time with each other and look for opportunities to be around one another. Do activities the other person enjoys as well. Make time for each other even when busy.

*Be the strength to each other's weakness.

*Character is important, both of you should have strong character.

*Always be honest with how the other person is treating you and how it makes you feel. Learn to be attentive and take their advice in how to change and speak to one another.

*Continue to stay friends with others, but make sure the way the relationship operates in support of a new relationship. (No one-on-one with opposite sex). Communicate about your locations, distance, and whereabouts.

*Don't live a single lifestyle anymore, don't party and drink or put yourself in a place where things can happen outside of your control and affect the relationship. Don't leave room for misunderstandings. Keep space between you and members of the opposite sex.

*Wait for marriage to have sex. When married, wait for each other to give willingly of themselves out of trust (this is mainly for those who have traumatic pasts and will be walking through new habits, etc.).

*Stay faithful to one another. Keep the relationship strong. Rely on one another. Handle problems, but always communicate on how to solve the problem.

*Don't forget your promises. Keep your word, and when misunderstandings come, talk it through, and be responsible for your mistakes.

*Create places for one another to have hobbies, an area to rest that is safe, and bring what is best for the other person into your own life plans.

*Show that you're trustworthy by way of action. Show that

you are dependable, always there for the other, and be strong and able to stand by their side in support.

*The man should be protective, but also learn to trust her. The woman should learn to step back and let him protect too.

*Watch how you communicate. Make sure it's not harsh, and be careful of the words and tone that are used.

*Take time to celebrate holidays and special occasions. Travel and get into nature, be there for each other's big events.

*When jealous, or when other feelings come into the relationship, communicate the reasons and make necessary changes on both sides.

*Respect your parents, learn how to navigate respecting them and being obedient while also being together. Prove yourself to both parents. (If obeying parents mean disobeying the Father, communicate to parents why you can't obey in this area, but that you love them.)

*Feel bad when you hurt the other's feelings, then make it right. Love each other in word and deed. Let your love blossom and grow closer, talk deeper, and invest more of yourselves into the relationship.

*Don't rush the adventure of being with each other, but enjoy the time. Don't lead each other on, always be open and honest.

*Make sure you each have a voice. Work together for the outcome. Be confident and don't let others change your worth and value.

*Learn to trust one another with your deepest secrets, be upfront about family background and situations, friends, health, your past, etc.

*Don't rely on phone calls, emails, and text messaging. Learn to communicate face to face.

*Don't please to impress. Instead, always keep them in mind, pray for them, dream together, follow the Holy Spirit, and continually confirm your heart and love through action and words.

*When life gets busy and stressful, pull away together to relax and rest in the Father.

*Take time to clarify situations, especially when feeling hurt. Don't assume a person means the worst thing.

*Don't put yourself in compromising situations with others. Especially because of photoshopping and AI—your character needs to be known.

*If your hints of liking someone are not understood, be brave and say it out loud and clear. Your hints should be clear and concise, leaving nothing to imagination.

*Find out each other's likes and dislikes by asking and observing.

*You should be free to be yourself and accepted for who you are. And even though you accept each other as you are, you should continue to encourage each other to be better and more like Jesus, aligned with who the Father made you to be.

*Ask questions.

*Be wise regarding counsel and who you seek advice from.

*See the details the Father is doing and make note of what He is saying in your relationship.

*Flirting during dating should not be sexual in nature or cause misunderstandings about your character and relationship.

*Teasing and pranks when dating and married should never make a person uncomfortable, cause pain and misunderstandings, or open the door for satan to speak lies into the relationship. Divorce, affairs, abandonment, and physical harm must never be used or spoken in any teasing, pranks, or arguments.

*When dating and engaged, do not awaken physical love and temptation. The world should not be able to question your character and relationship with the Father.

Insights for marriage and family relationships.

*Keep the romance alive.

*Flirting when married can be sexual and demonstrate desire.

*What would happen if we stayed connected through the married years, if we continued to pursue each other, and balanced life better? What would marriages be like? What would happen to divorce rates and affairs? What would happen if we took care of our bodies, kept up outward appearances, and continued allowing our bodies to keep the attraction going? How does our relationship with the Father and the Trinity affect our relationships?

*Share the household responsibilities. Learn to do them together, creating a fun and romantic atmosphere while you work hard on maintaining your home. Go grocery shopping together, do life together.

*If plans don't work out like you thought, change up the plan to create a new happy memory. Don't miss opportunities to love on one another.

*Be supportive and hold each other accountable. Share experiences so we don't have to repeat the same mistakes.

*Stand up for your relationship and fight for it.

*Have the freedom to cry, laugh, and feel around each other.

*Give comfort (hug) when needed, don't ever push away.

*Don't lose your compassion for your spouse. Learn to read each other, being aware of looks, facial expressions, and your spouse's nonverbal cues.

"¹⁵ Let the peace of Christ rule in your hearts, since as members of one body you were called to peace. And be thankful. ¹⁶ Let the message of Christ dwell among you richly as you teach and admonish one another with all wisdom through psalms, hymns, and songs from the Spirit, singing to God with gratitude in your hearts. ¹⁷ And whatever you do, whether in word or deed, do it all in the name of the Lord Jesus, giving thanks to God the Father through him."

(Colossians 3:15-17 NIV)

Chapter 39

In order for the blueprints of relationships to work the way the Father intends and for this ancient key to be unlocked in your life, it is of utmost importance that you have freedom, healing, and intimacy with the Father.

I want to discuss how, through the journey, each scenario is about the response and actions of the individual. Which means it's not about the scenario, but the heart. You may have found yourself in a similar situation, (though different details), where your responses, actions, and even how you felt when something was done to you, to be familiar in your heart. You might even think that I was reading your mail. But the truth is, the Holy Spirit put what I experienced in my own failed marriage and past relationships with others, in the journey and He just used different details. However, He also revealed to me that many believers struggle with and in relationships because of the heart. They may struggle with specific sins and habits, or have experienced their own traumas and wounds that have caused them to have similar feelings and emotions, habits, and a faulty belief system as I once had.

As you have journeyed with me, hearing the conversation between the Holy Spirit and I, I have prayed that you will discern and know how to apply the blueprint to your own relationships, and that you will allow the Holy Spirit to search your own heart for areas that you need healing and freedom in. We each have a part to play in relationship, meaning it's not just one person. Relationships take two individuals, and each one needs the Holy Spirit to search their heart, help them grow, and walk in this ancient blueprint.

If you are finding that you need spiritual healing and that your relationship with the Father and the Trinity has experienced a fallout, then it is time to rekindle your relationship with both. I would encourage you to get my book, 'Beyond Held Hostage'. This book was written by the leading of the Holy Spirit, and within its pages is the blueprint that the Father took me through for my own spiritual healing and breakthrough. 'Beyond Held Hostage,' reveals how we can have a relationship with the Trinity the way the Father has always longed for it to be. It will take you back to the Word (Bible) and create the firm foundation that you will need for earthly relationships.

Many of you might have also realized that you are in need of sexual healing and freedom. Perhaps you have fallen into sexual sin and self-pleasure, or perhaps you have trauma connected to sex and need the Father to redeem that. It is important to have steps in place that will help you on this journey. I've provided a list of some steps that you can incorporate, but I would also encourage you to find biblically-based counseling and/or teachings to help you on this journey. You may have a sexual addiction that needs to be broken off of you.

*Guard what you think about, especially regarding what triggers your body.

*Remove books, movies, etc. that bring temptation or thoughts that are not pleasing to the Father.

*Shut every door that was opened to satan, whether through music, pictures, movies, etc. Get rid of everything that is demonic and contrary to the Father.

*Command the demons and memories of a space to be removed in the name of Jesus, and ask the Holy Spirit to clean out the area and invite Him to dwell within. (My bedroom was a place of trauma, so I applied this step and it became a place of healing.)

*Workout daily and exhaust your body. Learn what cools down your body when desire arises.

*When desires contrary to the Father come, then pray in tongues, read the Word (Bible), and listen to the Holy Spirit.

These are just a few steps. As I said, it is important to find individuals who are godly and will hold you accountable. Find prayer warriors who can stand with you.

No matter what stage of relationship you are in, the Father has a journey for you to take as well. Press into the Holy Spirit and learn to navigate the blueprints of relationship with Him. He has given us an ancient key to relationships, but it is up to us to unlock the door, walk through, and apply it.

Chapter 40

"Aubrey." I could hear a smirk in the Holy Spirit's voice.

"Yes, Holy Spirit." A smile tugged at my lips.

"You thought I was done, didn't you?" He was teasing me now, and I giggled, knowing He had caught me. I truly thought I was done with writing forth what He had given me, but in this moment, I realized it wasn't true. He wasn't done, and there was something more that He was wanting me to impart to you. "You are right, I assumed that You were done, but I can sense in my spirit that I am wrong. There is something more You want me to write. Even though this journey has finished all the editing stages, I can't leave this part out."

"Aubrey, I want you to write a letter to the one who is reading about your journey with Me. Speak forth what I give you, and trust Me." There was no judgment in His voice, only a deep love.

My smile spread across my face as my spirit responded immediately with, "Yes, Holy Spirit. I will obey."

***

Dear Traveler,

You didn't pick up this book by accident. No, the Holy Spirit brought you to this book, in ways that only He could do. He brought the details together, and aligned your divine connection with perfect accuracy according to the Father's will.

Today, the Father, Yeshua, and the Holy Spirit want you to know that you are loved beyond words. You were created, formed perfectly in the womb, not as an afterthought, but as an answer. You are the answer to the problems of this world, and as you include the Trinity in your life, you become a weapon against the foul demons who hate that we were created to torture them.

The Father longs for you to go deeper and higher with Him, and as you are enveloped by His love to the extent that your every day life radiates Yeshua, the relationships here on earth are forever transformed into Kingdom relationships that will transcend time and reach into Heaven.

Many of you may have experienced failed relationships and friendships, and because of those failed attempts, you fear the ancient key the Father is given you. For some of you it might not have failed, but instead it became the place where you were abused, hurt, abandoned, shamed, and destroyed. The very idea of going into another relationship loses its joy, and instead you are filled with dread. Perhaps some of you have had good relationships, but the Father wants them to be Kingdom relationships.

Today, choose not to let fear hold you back from this ancient key. Declare truth over your perspective of relationship, begin to cultivate a heart of forgiveness and boldness, and as you forgive others (maybe even yourself) begin to ask the Holy Spirit how He wants to lead you in your relationships. Allow the Father to heal your heart, mind, soul, and to strengthen your spirit. Prayer is a powerful weapon that opens up the spiritual realm and prepares the physical realm for the change. As you fight on your knees, listen closely to His voice, be discerning, wise, full of the Father's presence, and as you do, begin to walk out what He shows you. Don't take your time, obedience should never be delayed, but acted upon immediately.

To those who are married: One of the hardest things in life is to be married to someone who won't let the Holy Spirit be a part of their life. Although it's hard, you must continue to be obedient and remain open to the Holy Spirit, get a couple of individuals (Same sex as you, or a married couple) who will make it a priority to stand in faith and pray with you for your spouse to respond to the Holy Spirit.

The Father, Yeshua, and the Holy Spirit love you so very deeply. The relationship They long to have with you compels

Them to persistently pursue you. Let yourself be caught. Instead of running away from Them, run to Them. Watch as everything changes, and how those changes affect the relationships you are longing for, waiting on, or even experiencing now. What you do now in the present will affect your future.

Dear Traveler, don't stop. Continue to fight for your relationships, walk in spirit instead of flesh, and be a walking key that opens ancient doors, realigning the Bride with her Bridegroom.

(A word from the Holy Spirit that I received for you on February 18, 2024.)

"For so long, you have been longing for and dreaming of a relationship that would change everything. Many tears have flowed as you have waited for your Tribe, a family, a spouse, and while some of those have been fulfilled, you are still waiting for the fulfillment of the Father's promises for all.

"Child, hold tight to the Father. Keep trusting and dreaming with Him. He is faithful and He will fulfill all that He has spoken and promised you.

"In the waiting, you have learned to protect, guard, and cultivate kingdom relationships. This time of waiting isn't in vain or useless, for the Father has been molding you, filling you with His presence, taking you through the fire to refine your character. Continue to pursue the Father and the Trinity. Pursue Us and you won't be disappointed.

"The time is approaching for the answer to your prayers to be activated in the physical realm. Prepare and get ready. Walk in faith and trust in the Father and in Us."

Blessings,

The Trinity and Aubrey Dawn Weinzetl

Epilogue

I was once again Philip-Transported to the garden of my heart. In shock, I looked around and realized all the walls had been removed. Every hibiscus flower was vibrant in color and variety. Not a single one was black and white. I admired the beauty of the flowers until my eyes drifted beyond them and to where the walls once stood.

Standing on the diabase rock, I saw that the view beyond my garden was that of the heavens. But not like the heavens I recognized. Within this space burst forth bright colors of light, creating a brilliant display of luminescence. As I watched the scene unfold before me, I saw angels moving about, many headed down to the spiritual realm to war with the enemy.

Surprise hit me. 'Why? Why is the garden of my heart here?' I wondered silently. Aloud, I asked, "Holy Spirit, why am I here?"

"Aubrey."

I turned at the sound of my Father's voice.

"Daddy? Why is the garden of my heart located here?"

"You are not from earth. The garden of your heart, your spirit, is waiting for the day that you return to Me in Heaven. The garden of your heart is not found in earth, nor does it belong there. Your spirit connects with the Holy Spirit, transcends beyond the earthly realm, is given understanding of the spiritual realm, and thus, you enter into My presence in Heaven. Every time you communicate in Tongues with Us, your spirit is Philip-Transported to where We lead.

"Because I am your center, I envelop your heart. The Holy Spirit dwells within you, and My Son, Yeshua, will one day soon be coming to bring you back home. The diabase rock you stand on is a symbol of Me. In Psalms 71:3 (NIV) says, '3 Be my rock of refuge, to which I can always go; give the command to save me, for you are my rock and my fortress.' I am your refuge, and as you stand in Me, I will make you victorious and a conqueror over everything satan throws at you.

"You belong in the spiritual realm in Heaven with Me. Therefore, as you live in the world, you have the feeling of a deep knowing beyond what your earthly mind can grasp. You function in and have authority that comes from Me in Heaven, not from earth. Therefore, as you draw closer and closer to Me in relationship, you go beyond what is seen in the physical realm and are given understanding of the heavenlies.

"My Daughter, I have removed every wall that we built to protect you during these three years. Now it is time for you to step out and pursue love once again. Do not fear or worry about making the same mistakes, because this time you are in covenant relationship with Me, you listen to My voice, and you give the Holy Spirit access to your days. Guard your heart against the enemy, but be vulnerable and open with the one I am sending to you. Do not close yourself off from him, do not build a wall between you and he, do not view him as the same as your ex for he is not your ex-husband; and DO keep step with the Holy Spirit.

"Your heart is now open to allow in the one I have for you. You are healthy now and ready for a relationship. Stay in Me and I will lead you through the uncharted waters of my new wineskin relationships.

"Daughter, I am placing a diamond necklace around your neck as a symbol of how you have been adorned spiritually, mentally, and physically. You are now ready to be presented for 'your night with the king', and the future I have for you both."

"Let it begin, Father."

"12 "Look, I am coming soon! My reward is with me, and I will give to each person according to what they have done. 13 I am the Alpha and the Omega, the First and the Last, the Beginning and the End."

Revelations 22:12-13 (NIV)

References:

Aaron Earls, "7 in 10 Women Who Have Had an Abortion Identify as a Christian." 2021. https://research.lifeway.com/2021/12/03/7-in-10-women-who-have-had-an-abortion-identify-as- a-christian/

Aubrey Dawn Weinzetl, "Beyond Held Hostage". Published by Aubrey Dawn Weinzetl. 2023

Biblical Archaeology Society Staff, "Daily Life in Ancient Israel". 2023. https://www.biblicalarchaeology.org/daily/ancient-cultures/ancient-israel/daily-life-in-ancient-israel/

John Thorington, "Porn in the Church-a Study." 2020. https://www.restoringheartscounseling.com/2020/12/21/is-porn-addiction-a-problem-in-your-church/

Lawrence B. Finer, PhDa. "Trends in Premarital Sex in the United States, 1954–2003," 2007. https://www.ncbi.nlm.nih.gov/pmc/articles/PMC1802108/

Muhammad, "Quran." Translated by Al-Baqarah. 2024. https://quran.com/en/al-baqarah/191

Muhammad, "Quran." Translated by Yusuf Ali. 2024. https://quran.com/9/5?translations=18,85,84,21,20,19,101,22,17,95

Author Biography and Contact

Aubrey Dawn Weinzetl lives in the beautiful state of South Dakota. Her relationship with the Father, Jesus, and Holy Spirit is an integral part of her life.

Before becoming an author and speaker, Aubrey graduated from Rocky Mountain College of Art and Design with a Degree of Bachelor of Fine Arts in Interior Design (Magna Cum Laude). Most of her years of work have been spent imparting hope and truth to children, working as an interior designer at a locally owned furniture store, as well as helping raise her nephew and niece.

Aubrey enjoys being with family, traveling, experiencing other cultures, being out in nature, reading, listening to music, and most importantly helping others find hope and breakthrough in their own lives.

If you would like to have Aubrey Dawn Weinzetl come and speak at a Bible Study, conference, event, etc., want to know when her next book will come out, hear about opportunities to hear her in person and the events she will be doing; please visit her at:

Website: **www.aubreydw.com**
Facebook: **https://www.facebook.com/AubreyDawnWeinzetl**
Email: **Aubrey.heldhostage@gmail.com**
Youtube: **https://www.youtube.com/@AubreyDawnWeinzetl**
Instagram: **https://www.instagram.com/aubreydawnweinzetl/**